S0-BYJ-889

This book is dedicate to Carole Sarkan,
who believed that I could write a book.

And also to Iris Lucas,
for helping me to learn how to wander
outside of my box.

"The Ghost Journal"
Memoirs of a Ghost Tour Guide in Williamsburg, Virginia

Emily Christoff Flowers

4th Printing

2012

Front Cover by the Author

Copyright 2012 by Lulu

Printed in the United States

ISBN – 978-1-105-65958-4

Contents

These are the real stories of a tour guide working in Williamsburg, Virginia.

Photo by Shelley Thacker Millirons, 2009

The views on the occult and the supernatural in this book are not necessarily those of the owners of the Manor House

Chapter One

My Journey Begins

My name is Emily but most people just call me Em. Somehow I found myself working as a ghost tour guide at a private plantation home in Virginia. It was just one of those jobs that I sort of stumbled into without giving it much thought, but looking back, it seems sort of amazing that all of this crazy stuff happened to me. After all, I am just a normal wife and mom, living a normal middle class life in a small suburban home with my husband, kids and pets. The highlight of my week usually involves making a roast and watching a good movie on the T.V. Why the ghosts come to me is a total mystery. Maybe they are attracted by my mundane life.

It occurred to me one day that someone might enjoy hearing my stories, so I wrote them all down into this little journal. Oh, and just so you know, the stories are real. At least they sure seem real to me. I know that you are sitting there rolling your eyes, but I did not make this stuff up, I swear. Before you dig into my tales though, I would like to explain how I met my ghost friends.

I vividly remember the day that I first saw the old "haunted" Manor House. It was September 11th of 2006. I was hired to draw portraits and teach art classes at a 300 and something year old plantation turned resort in Williamsburg, Virginia. I had just finished a grueling and exhaustive career drawing profile faces outdoors at a local amusement park, and I was starting this new art job in a desperate hope that I could begin over again somewhere a little less stressful.

The timeshare was huge, hosting thousands of visitors during the summer months, and I was excited to be working there. As I drove down the tree lined entrance to the resort I gaped as I approached the massive 270 year old brick structure which dominated the landscape. It was stunning as it sat proudly under the shade of the immense oak and magnolia trees.

The first time that I entered the colonial mansion I had an overwhelming feeling that I was being greeted by a silent host. In the early morning gloom the house seemed apprehensive as if it was holding its breath. As my hand touched the front door my hair stood on end. I felt an anxious tightening in my chest. I reluctantly gathered my art supplies and continued into the dark front hall.

My new manager had informed me that for the first part of the work day I would sit at my easel under the grand staircase on the bottom floor as I waited for guests to arrive to have their portraits drawn. The other half of the day I would spend up on the third floor art studio teaching vacationing guests simple arts and craft classes. I would teach basket making, metal embossing and beginning watercolor classes as well as a few other simple things that she thought the tourists might enjoy. She also reminded me that I was to keep the lights off on the bottom two floors at all times so that we don't fade the furniture. I set my up my easel in the shadowy front hall and settled in. It was perfect.

I loved my new job. It was so much better than standing on a crowded street corner hawking my sketches with the roar of a roller coaster looming over me, and sweat turning the chalk on my face and hands into mud. At the park I had to draw my portraits in 5 minutes, but at the resort I could work at my own pace and spend time talking and schmoozing with my models. I love to talk, or at least that is what my husband says. I wasn't creating masterpieces, but I was working in the air conditioning and so I was very happy. I was also falling in love with the manor house. It was almost as if it was a living thing, with a gentle yet charismatic personality all of its own.

As the days and weeks flowed by I started to notice some very odd things about the place. If I happened to glance up at the staircase I might see some strange flickering shadows flying quickly towards the second floor out of the corner of my eye. I

2

began hearing heavy footsteps on the old hard wood floors, but when I would run into that room it would be empty of all but dust.

Many mornings I felt absolutely sure that someone was standing right behind me as I was doodling at my easel, but I would turn around just to see that I was alone in the dark foyer. I swear, it was almost as if I could feel their breath on the back of my neck, as if they were just about to reach out and touch my shoulder with dry, cold fingers. I thought that maybe I was feeling anxious because I was not used to working in such a quiet place, and the silence was getting to me. You know, anxiety can sure do strange things to a person.

One morning as I was lumbering up the first flight of stairs, my arms full of art supplies, I was dumb struck by the sight of a full body black shadow of a ghost calmly walking across the second floor foyer. He didn't have a care in the world and just ignored me. I stood rooted to the spot, my mind in turmoil as I watched him disappear into the library. Once I was able to breathe again I followed him into the room. My heart sunk when I realized that there was no one there. What the heck!

I was scared out of my wits, but I needed this job, so instead of running away I ran up to the studio and slammed the door behind me. I prayed that whatever it was would leave me alone, and I urged my hands to stop shaking.

I was hesitant to ask my new manager about what I had just seen, since I didn't want her to think that I was off my rocker, but after several days of deliberation I finally gathered the courage to look Belinda in the eye and ask her if the house was haunted. She took a long look at me, as if weighing her answer. I was embarrassed and certain that my face was bright red, but I stood my ground. I held my breath as I waited for her to start laughing, but she surprised me by calmly admitting that it was true. The Manor House is haunted. In fact, she even talks to them by name. You could have knocked me over with a feather.

She told me that the primary ghost's name is Eliza. The house also hosts the desolate Lady of the woods, a male servant named Gus, a slew of Civil War soldiers, a strict plantation master, and something nasty in the basement. Belinda did not believe in ghosts until she began working in the manor house, but now she was as certain of their presence as she was of her own existence. I asked if anyone had ever documented them or written down the details of the sightings. She seemed shocked at the idea. No way, why would we do that? How silly!

In fact, he went on to tell meme that I was not allowed to ever speak about this to anyone, or I could lose my job. If a guest asked me about ghosts I was to deny them and change the subject. I guess our spooks were a dirty little secret. I asked her why she wanted to hide them from the public, and she just rolled her eyes and said in a condescending voice, "You don't want them to think you are crazy do you?" Well, no, I guess didn't.

She also said that she didn't want those types of people in her house, and that it would be disrespectful to turn it into a haunted attraction. She was sure that people wouldn't respect a historic home if we talk about their ghosts.

For the next few months when someone asked me if the house was haunted, I would just shrug my shoulders and say, 'Oh, maybe it is, maybe it isn't." Fortunately my lie didn't stop the ghosts and me from getting to know one another very well after a while. I forgot to mention to my new boss that I am horrible about keeping secrets.

As the months progressed so did my job. I was eventually promoted to supervisor and given more responsibilities. My co-workers started to come to me with whispers of their own ghost sightings, and for some reason visitors also approached me with questions and their own observations. It was almost as if these witnesses were drawn to me for this very purpose. I soon grew tired of denying the truth and began to speak to our visitors about Eliza and the other ghosts as if they were real, when my manager wasn't around. I was no longer referred to as the resort artist; I was called the "Ghost Lady". I kind of liked that. I figured that if I was going to be fired for being honest, then so be it.

4

Belinda eventually moved on to another job and was replaced by Iris. My new boss had been working in the house for almost 20 years and had a deep love and devout respect for the home. Unlike my first manager, she didn't mind when I discussed the spirits with the guests, in fact she encouraged it.

One day, when Iris and I were strolling through the dusty rooms together, and sharing some of our ghost stories, a few visitors started listening to us and Iris hammed it up. She really put on a show, and the audience loved it and rewarded her with applause, which she followed with a curtsy.

As I stood back and enjoyed my new manager's antics it suddenly occurred to me that it would be a really cool activity to walk through the house and tell some of our personal ghost stories with our resort guests on a regular basis. I didn't want to dishonor the house by making up things and having actors jump out of dark corners, I thought it should be honest, sincere and respectful. I also thought that we should discuss our own plantation's history and our own ghosts specifically. I didn't want to just engage in yet another generic discussion about the ghosts of Williamsburg, which we tried before, and which had become a bit overdone by this point. Iris became so excited when I mentioned the idea to her that she immediately handed the project over to me. The Ghost Tours were born.

To be quite honest with you, I was not thrilled with the assignment. I didn't mean to insinuate that I should be the one to do the stupid tour; I thought she would hire some vendor. One of these days I should learn to keep my big mouth shut around Iris when I get one of my brilliant ideas, but now I was stuck with it.

Please keep in mind that I am not a historian, a paranormal investigator, or a writer. I knew that I had a lot of studying to do, because nothing in art school had prepared me for writing and giving a ghost tour. I had never even been on one. All I have ever done my entire adult life was to live, eat, breathe and sleep art, and I was quite obsessive about my career. I couldn't understand why she wouldn't just let me draw my portraits and teach my craft classes. This would be my first venture outside of my "art" box, and it made me squirm. When I begged her to reconsider putting me in charge of this crazy idea she just laughed at me and said no way, you were meant to do this.

After a few more failed attempts to talk Iris out of doing the project I reluctantly started researching for the tour. I knew I needed to study history as well as the science of ghost hunting, but where to begin? I was clueless, frustrated, and I hated history.

I am a bit embarrassed to say that because I hated history I knew almost nothing of the local history of Williamsburg. Much to my surprise, the more I discovered, the more excited I became. I gobbled up everything I could read, and slowly began to feel a beautiful sense of pride growing within me for this amazing farm, nestled on ground zero of the birth of our great nation.

Some of the research that I did was on line, but I focused on reputable web sites. I was also very fortunate to have the acquaintance of a young man with a love of research. Our gardener, Matthew, spent long hours in the library just for fun. You gotta be pretty smart to want to spend hours in a library just for fun!

The ghost stories were much easier to put together than the history. I started by writing down every personal experience I could recall. When I ran out of memories I just started interviewing all of my co-workers who were willing to talk to me about it. I have included here all of the accounts that were told to me with sincerity, whether or not I personally believed them to be paranormal. You will be glad to know that I am not sharing the drunken ramblings of tourists who might have had a bit too much sun and beer that day, although I find those stories to be quite entertaining.

Once I started giving the tours my experiences with the ghosts occurred almost weekly. I think that the presence from all of us in the house was stirring them up somehow. My collection of stories soon became too big to keep in a simple journal and

6

described in one hour. Our visitors were clamoring for more information, so after several months of simply e-mailing the journal I decided to just write a book. I am very limited on time on the tours and do not go into the historical depth that the mansion deserves, and only share about a third of the ghost stories during my one hour, so hopefully this book will fill in some of those gaps. And kids, you will get a thorough dose of history along with all of the scary stuff, whether you like it or not.

Please understand that In order to protect the privacy of my co-workers and my place of employment I have omitted last names and changed the first names of a few of the witnesses. Although the house is actually open to the public for tours and such, I am also not mentioning the name of our resort, so that we are not bombarded by curious ghost seekers. I will simply tell you that it is in the middle of the historic triangle of Williamsburg, that it is beautiful, and that it is quite haunted.

Photo of orbs in front of the house, by Shelley Thacker Millirons

Manor House, Emily Christoff Flowers, 2011

What is a Ghost?

I'm going to tell you a secret. When I was 13 years old I thought that I had seen a ghost. I woke around three in the morning to the site of a shadow of a tall man walking around my bedroom. He bent over my belongings strewn about the floor and then slowly walked over to where I was trembling in my bed. He reached his hand out and gently touched my Led Zeppelin poster hanging on the wall. He bent his face close to mine. I could feel the air stir from his body. I could see his shadow block the faintly lit ceiling. I could hear him as he passed in front of the dehumidifier that we kept outside of my door. He wasn't evil, just very curious.

I told my family and friends about it but no one believed me. In fact, my 6 siblings had a blast making fun of me for my childish imagination, and I wished that I had kept it to myself. Unfortunately, even then I had a big mouth.

Eventually I concluded that if modern science had not proven the existence of ghosts by 1981, then what I saw must not have been real. It was much easier to convince myself at that young age that ghosts didn't exist, than to accept ridicule.

However, when I saw the shadow man in the manor house 25 years later, I was a full grown middle aged woman with three teenage kids of my own. I was no longer a scared adolescent afraid of shifting forms hiding in the dark corners of my closet. Certainly science had to have some sort of explanation by now, and I was bound and determined to find out what it was. I started asking myself questions and reading, in hopes of finding logical answers.

What happens after we die? Do we simply cease to exist or do we survive in some form? Is death the end? It is a great mystery, one sooner or later we are all forced to face. All religions believe that our bodies are just the vessel to hold our soul, and that it carries on after our death. Philosophers and scientists have also puzzled over this for thousands of years, and now they claim to be closing in on the answers. I wondered if the soul is just a myth or one of the fundamental elements of the universe yet to be defined by science.

I read that the word paranormal simply means that an event is not in accordance of scientific laws of that time. If you experience something paranormal this does not mean that you just saw a ghost, it means that you just saw something unexplainable by science. This makes the topic of life after death a paranormal issue.

For example, educated Europeans supposedly thought that the earth was flat. Columbus allegedly sought to disprove this theory when he set out to sail around the world. Until this theory was later supported by European science, Columbus's theory was considered paranormal. Of course some people knew long before the time of Columbus that the earth was a sphere, but guess what? No one believed them! They were often ridiculed and sometimes even punished for their belief.

Is my brother right? Am I crazy, or do ghosts have a scientific explanation? I may never know for certain, but the longer I worked in the house, the more I became a true believer that I was sharing the gloomy, decomposing mansion with intelligent unseen beings of some kind.

If you are the type of person who likes to label and categorize everything then you will appreciate knowing that most researchers tend to lump ghosts into two major groupings. I understand that sometimes the things that we interpret as an intelligent haunt of some unfortunate human soul is actually just a lingering manifestation of energy which has left its imprint on the house. The professionals call this first sort of activity a residual haunting, or a psychic recording. I try to think of it as an actual play back of time or an echo of a person's energy from long ago. In fact, if you look at it this way it is not actually a ghost, it's more like watching a video. I suspect that this may describe many of our sightings throughout the years. This farm land has been filled not only with tragedy but also with love, compassion and joy for centuries, and we are bound to pick up on some of this positive energy, as well as some of the more horrific. (Balzano, 26)

According to most investigators the second type of spirit, called an intelligent ghost, is the remaining soul of an actual human who died, and who is attempting to communicate with the living. Being an intelligent ghost does not mean that Eliza has a high IQ, it just means that she can see us but we can't see her. She knows that we are here and she most definitely has a strong opinion about us and wishes to communicate her thoughts and feelings with the living. She has a relationship with her surroundings and with the people who have invaded her world.

Many modern day paranormal investigators will also include a third category, which describes the non-human entity. This is actually the energy of a demonic spirit or perhaps an angel as described in the bible and other religious texts. When I think of this type of ghost I think of that movie where the little girl's head spins around and split pea soup gushes out of her mouth as she screams obscenities. We do not have any demons in the house thank goodness, but you got to admit that was a great movie.

Well, ok, so now that I knew more about ghosts, I wanted to know why they would be lurking in our manor house. I soon learned that one reason an intelligent ghost may hang about a place is because as a living soul they were in love with their home and can't suffer to part with it after death. I also understand that if a person has endured a traumatic ending they might not go into the light. This could be because they may not realize that they are dead, they have unfinished business, or they might fear that they will go to hell for participating in the inevitable horrors of war. This explains perfectly why our house is haunted, and why it is so important to know its history. As you will soon learn, I have discovered that many people have died tragically in and around the house, and it seems that their spirits may be lingering here.

C 1930 – 1942, Source unknown

Chapter Two

The Ghosts of Jamestown

Now that we know what a ghost is, it is time to introduce our ghosts to you in more detail. I was beginning to understand that paranormal investigation and history are so closely intertwined, that you cannot study one without the other, so let's just start from the beginning.

I soon grew to love our local past and spent hours reading, researching and asking smart people questions about our earliest settlers and Native Americans. Many of our ghosts are believed to have come from events that happened on this land centuries ago, long before the house was even built in 1735. If you were to stroll through this area before Jamestown was settled in 1607, you would have seen open corn fields, lush forests, peaceful villages of Native American long houses surrounded by steaming, mosquito infested swamps.

Before the House Was Built

In case you don't know what happened when our nation's first permanent English settlement was established, let's give a quick refresher course for beginners, shall we? It is important to know this stuff because our farm was part of Jamestown at that time. I promise to keep it brief and will refrain from passing out tests at the end of this chapter.

Before the Europeans settled Jamestown, the peaceful Tsenacommacah, an alliance of Algonquian-speaking natives, lived here on these gently rolling hills. The Powhatan people were a large populous that covered the entire eastern coast of Virginia. Chief Powhatan, whose proper name was

13

Wahunsenacawh, was their great leader. He united 32 small villages into one large nation which he called the Powhatan Nation. In the earliest days of the English colony, this wonderful leader's first intent may have been to incorporate the newly landed English settlers into his nation as another tribe. The colonists had another agenda however, and forty years of war followed their landing. (Wood, 15)

The great king was quite the ladies' man, as he had at least one hundred wives. My husband says that he feels really sorry for him about that, and made some lame comment that he could hardly handle just one himself. King Powhatan had a beloved daughter named Matoaka. She was one of hundreds of his children, but she was his favorite. He gave her a nickname that in the Algonquian language meant "playful one" or "spoiled one". You may know her simply as Princess Pocahontas. She was his pet child.

I need to hit the pause button for a second here, and clear up a nasty rumor about our little princess. Contrary to popular belief Pocahontas did not marry Captain John Smith. They didn't even date or hold hands. Some historians doubt that the story of her saving his life by covering Smith's body with her own, just as her father was going to brain him was true either. She was not a sexy 21 year old woman with long flowing hair and a pet raccoon when she met him; she was around the age of 11. The front of her head was most likely shaved, and her naked body covered in bear grease and tattoos. (Rasmussen, 50) You would not have seen her on the cover of Colonial Glamour Magazine back then, at least not until she became older.

Pocahontas did however become a regular visitor to Jamestown as a child and would have been very familiar with the swamp land that eventually became our plantation. She became an envoy between the two cultures and made the 12 mile hike to Jamestown once a month or so. She converted to Christianity after being held hostage by the English, and married John Rolfe, the first settler to bring tobacco to the new world. She died at the age of 21 while visiting his family in England.

Captain John Smith was Pocahontas's friend and also a leader of Jamestown during the earliest years. Please remember that although a current cartoon musical about her life was a great fantasy romance, and beautifully illustrated, it was highly glamorized and far from the truth. I feel much better after having clarified that rumor, thanks for letting me rant. (PBS, 4)

Anyhow, before I digressed, I was saying that we found evidence of her and Smith's people here on the property, which may explain some of our ghost sightings. An interview from the Virginia Gazette, dated June 12, 1942, claimed that a farmer named Mr. Slauson found the remains of an old grist mill on this land. He believed that this was the legendary mill built by Captain John Smith on the Powhatan creek. The farmer noted that sometime in late 1930s, workmen were building a concrete bridge across the creek, and they found two of the old millstones which identified the site of the mill. Nothing remains of this mill today.

I have a very interesting story that indicates that Captain Smith's specter may have made a visit to the plantation in recent years. Maybe he is looking for his lost mill. (Virginia Gazette, 1942)

The Ghost of Captain John Smith

In 2007 a guest mailed us a peculiar photo of the Kitchen, which is a separate building sitting next to the house. They claimed that they took a photo during an early morning walk and that no one was in the Kitchen at the time. When they got home, and enlarged their photos, they could see the face of a bearded man wearing a high ruffled collar in the upstairs window staring out at them. He looks like he is wearing clothing from around the time that Jamestown was settled.

When we first examined the photo we seriously doubted that the face was a ghost, since it could also easily be a bouquet of flowers or a candle stick. We also could tell that the photo was not taken in the morning as the witness claimed, based on the angle of the light, so we simply tucked the photo away and most of us forgot completely about it.

Several years later, as I was researching for the tours, I came across this beautiful etching of Captain John Smith on line, created in 1616 by artist Simon van de Passe. I spent some time studying the image, enjoying the lines and texture of the piece, but something really nagged me about it. I had seen this same pose, face and composition somewhere else.

This photo was taken by a guest showing an odd face in the window. I have enlarged and reversed the window and placed it next to an image of the engraving done by artist Simon van de Passe of Captain John Smith, in 1616

Fortunately Iris kept the old photo of the ghost of the kitchen. I scanned it into my computer and enlarged the face in the window, viewing both the image of the "ghost" and the etching of Smith side by side. They were identical. The beard, buttons, collar, angle of the shoulder and hand were all almost exactly the same. The only difference was that the photo was in color and in reverse of the etching. Smith is described as having red hair. The man in the photo has a red beard. The portrait artist in me could not deny the similarities between the image and the portrait. It made chills run down my back. Either this was a sighting of the captain, a remarkable coincidence, or a very

16

elaborate hoax. Why don't you take a look at the photos and tell me what you think?

Cannibals in the Swamp, and Other Weird Stuff

After Jamestown was settled in 1607 it quickly grew into a fort surrounded by a radius of small farms and settlements. The main fort was less than four miles from where the manor house now stands, and so our plantation may have been occupied by a small farm next to Smith's grist mill, and would have been considered part of Jamestown.

Did you know that there was a horrible 2 year period of time in Jamestown called the "starvation time"? Most people don't know that according to legend, the settlers became cannibals in order to survive. Many stories have been passed down of hunger ravaged people digging up the remains of their loved ones in order to endure. It is documented that one man was hung for shooting his pregnant wife for the purpose of consuming her. 1 out of 10 colonists died, leaving only 57 survivors.

This was a very dark time for the farmers that lived in our murky swamp. I don't know about you, but if someone had dug up my remains and had them for dinner, I would haunt him just for revenge. That's just gross.

Jamestown eventually survived to become a thriving community, and is frequently referred to as the cradle of our great nation, but it came at a great cost of lives. Over the next four decades the Powhatan people and the settlers of Jamestown were at war. After this war was over there were several more years of raids called Bacon's Rebellion, where many thousands of innocent Native American men, women and children were slaughtered in their government protected reservations, by a group of rampaging settlers lead by Nathanial Bacon. During this time Jamestown was destroyed as well as the plantation next door, the governor's house at Green Spring Plantation. (Friends of Green Spring) Folklore has it that there was a cemetery at our plantation before the manor house was built, in which some of the condemned men from Bacon's Rebellion were laid to rest after behind hanged. That could definitely explain a few residual hauntings. (Lanciano)

It is commonly known that Chief Powhatan had a fort built very near Jamestown. Legend says that this fort was in the Powhatan swamp, and that the creek and swamp were named after the fort. An interview in an old newspaper states that farmer Slauson remembered finding this legendary fort deep in the swamp behind the house, when he first purchased the residence in 1903. At that time Slauson claimed that it was still in good shape. (Kibler,)

According to the recently retired head groundskeeper at the timeshare, a Native American fort of some kind may have been discovered on the property. One afternoon Gene came into my office to say hi and he sat down for a few minutes just to chit chat. I love picking Gene's brain. He is one smart cookie. Since he knew those woods like the back of his hand, I asked him if he ever saw anything out in the bogs that looked like a fort. He told me that he didn't know of a fort, but in the late 1990s a team of archeologists did a dig back by our swamp in preparation for the construction of a new jogging trail for the resort. They unearthed a huge stash of Native American relics.

Gene was curious where the dig was, so he hiked back there one afternoon and saw the holes. I promised him that I would not tell anyone where exactly the holes were, but he showed me how to find them on a map. It was exactly where Powhatan's fort was described by witnesses many years ago. Needless to say, the jogging trail idea was scrapped and Chief Powhatan's fort remains buried and hidden away in the middle of our extensive woods.

I know of no ghost sightings specifically of Pocahontas or her great father; however my good friend Lucy, who is a psychic, swears that she saw a residual haunting that involved many arrows on a slight hill between Eliza's grave and the Registration building. Later, a guest took a photo of this same spot and got an image on her camera of a glowing mist in the shape of a man with his hand raised as if in greeting. I saw the photo on her view finder, and it was very clear.

Engravings by artist Simon van de Passe, created in 1616. These are portraits of Captain John Smith and Pocahontas, after she converted to Christianity and was renamed Rebecca.

The Manor House , side view. 2011

Chapter Three

Building the Manor House

Before we go much farther I want to explain something to you. Our beautiful house was the second home built in the center of a massive southern plantation. This is not a secret. We should not deny this. There are many people who find the word "plantation" to be offensive. I personally feel that regardless of the ugliness of the past, it is vital to be honest with you, so I have chosen to use the word in order to remain truthful about our past. We have no right to change history just because we are embarrassed by the mistakes of our past.

I want so badly to tell you that this was not one of those types of plantations, but it was. This plantation did have slaves, as all southern plantations did. It is my personal choice to use this historically accurate word, and is in no way a reflection on the people who currently own the house and the resort. Please forgive me if you find my use of this word offensive. By the way, the legal name of the modern resort no longer contains the word "plantation", in order to avoid offense.

We have no available records of the very first settlers of the plantation, other than the legends of Smith's grist mill and Powhatan's fort. However, we do have record that in 1643 King Charles of England granted Richard and Benjamin Eggleston a thousand acre tract of land bordering on the Powhatan Swamp. They had a productive plantation and their family lived on the property for several generations in a farm house that has long since been swallowed by the swamp. Their granddaughter, Elizabeth, married a famous master architect named Richard Taliaferro. According to architectural historians, it was Taliaferro who built the Manor House around 1735 as his personal residence on the land that he was given in Elizabeth's dowry. Unfortunately official data about the house and farm from before the Civil War is lacking due to the destruction of the court house and the home, both casualties of this war. (Lanciano, 96)

Photo by Shelley Thacker Millirons, 2010

A Description of the House

The builder of our historical home was described by the President of the Executive Council of the colony as "our most skillful architect," and he was selected to make renovations to the Governor's Palace in Williamsburg in 1749. Many public buildings in Virginia have been documented as his design, including: President's House (College of William and Mary), Kingsmill, Abingdon Church, Christ Church (Lancaster County), Ampthill, Wilton, Blenheim, Carter's Grove, Charles City Court House, the Wythe house, and Sabine Hall. It is also believed that he built many more personal homes and public buildings than have been attributed to him; however, a full list of all of his accomplishments has long since been erased by time. (Lanciano, 371)

We do know for sure that as a young man Taliaferro built the manor house as his family home. It is a beautiful example of early American Georgian Architecture. This style can be described as being a simple one to two story box, two rooms deep and using strict symmetrical arrangements.

The Manor House is a very important home. The stately brick structure was accepted to the National Register of Historic Places and the Virginia Landmarks Register in 1970. This means that we cannot bulldoze the house and we must have permission to make any changes to the structure. (Lanciano, 166)

Let's take an imaginary walk around the house together before I continue with our ghosts, shall we? Remember, I'm an artist, not an architect, so this description will be as I observe the house, and not as a university archeology professor might describe it to you.

Standing in front of the house we notice that the building is backwards now. When it was first built archeologists believe that what we use as the front of the house now was the back of the house then. The front and the back are identical. Old Williamsburg road leading up to the house actually came from the opposite direction than what it does now, and has since changed names. This road is over 400 years old, and I have a wonderful ghost story to share about it a little later.

There are two massive chimneys, standing 60 feet high, with sides about 16 feet wide. They were originally built to service eight fireplaces, but currently the house is equipped with modern day air conditioning and heating systems. Although we no longer use the fireplaces, on some days you can still smell the hint of burning wood as you walk around the rooms. It is most likely just the wind blowing down the chimneys, but it is fun to think that it might be a residual ghost smell from a fire burning by a bedside from a time long ago. Once the smell was so intense that we actually called security to help us search for the fire, but we did not find one.

If you look closely at the left chimney you will see a cannon ball embedded into the brick. This was not shot at the house during battle, but was mortared there by one of the owners who found it on property, to honor the fallen soldiers who died nearby. We assume that many of these fallen casualties of war lay in unmarked graves near the house, since according to local folklore; the house may have been used as a war time hospital. Later my psychic friend Lucy will verify this.

Matt told me that construction workers have discovered a second cannon ball on the right chimney. He said that it appeared to be mortared in place, and is quite small. It is placed near the roof, and so you cannot see this artifact unless you are standing on the roof. I am not sure why anyone would place a cannon ball way up there where you can't see it, but it is pretty cool that it was found anyhow.

The brick is in Flemish bond and is 54 by 34 feet and is three stories high, with a basement that sits under the entire structure. The walls are 26 inches thick in the basement, 22 inches at the first floor and only 18 inches on the second floor. The third floor walls are all wooden.

We believed that the clay for the brick may have been dug near the house and fired right here on property, as was the custom of the day. Matt told me that the archeologists who did a dig around the house prior to the current renovation could not verify this however.

Every other brick has the remnants of a clear glaze. I understand that these were the bricks that were directly facing the fire as they were in the kiln; the heat melted the sand on the brick into a liquid glaze. Today this glaze looks like a peeling grey film, but centuries ago the visual effects of this glaze would have been astounding for colonists as they approached the plantation from the long road leading up to it. Visitors would have seen the house sparkling in the bright Virginia sunshine from miles away, surrounded by lush green fields of tobacco, prize winning horses and apple orchards.

Closer inspection of the brick shows that names have been carved onto the outside of the house. We have no way of authenticating these signatures; however it was not uncommon in early America for owners of a house and their distinguished guests to carve their names into the brick or etch them onto windows. The oldest carved date of 1643 was most likely inscribed when the house was first built, in memory of the original owners of the property. You can see this on the front of the house on the right side.

Canon Ball in the Chimney,
Emily Christoff Flowers 2012

Walking around to the right of the house you will see the Kitchen with a cute little herb garden next to it. This building is a reconstruction of the original kitchen, and was built in the early twentieth century. This building is very haunted, but we will get to that story a little later. When this was a working plantation the manor house would have been surrounded by many other outbuildings, such as smoke houses, dairy or horse barns, a circle of small huts for slaves, storages barns, chicken coops, various gardens, orchards, stocked fishing ponds and many other structures.

Next to the Kitchen is a reconstructed building that we call the General Store. It was built in 1984 and we use it today like a little 7-11. Near the Kitchen you will also see a well. It is fake, so don't try to jump down it, you won't get too far. The entrance to the creepy old basement is on this side of the house as well. I really don't want to go down there, but I guess we should if you want to see everything. I need to take a deep breath first and calm myself before I descend. I had a very bad experience down here a few years ago, and it still freaks me out.

The basement door is covered with a stained plastic curtain which opens to a narrow brick entrance. As you descend the air gets colder and thicker with the stench of old mold, and standing water. The cellar is all original, and so visitors especially enjoy going down into its dampness, just so they can see the true structure of the house.

The basement before the renovation. Emily Christoff Flowers, 2011

The first few times I went down, I felt sort of grossed out because the basement is smelly, dark and filled with nasty little spiders and squirmy things. It has small dirty windows, but since boxwood shrubs surround the house the light is very sporadic, and shifts as the sun filters through the leaves of the trees

The three rooms down here are the same shape and size as the rooms on the first floor. In fact the brick walls that divide the basement continue all the way up to the next floor. There is a low hanging wooden ceiling covered in spider webs, raw brick walls, and the floor still has some of the original brick from the time before the great fire. It really is quite impressive.

Arches in the walls support the large fireplaces on the floors above, and many times I thought I could see a shadow hiding in their gloom, peering at me with malevolent eyes. The arch immediately to the left of the front door has the remains of an old stove pipe in it. For this reason we speculate that the basement may have been used as a dining room at one time, or perhaps as a brewery for the famous Taliaferro hard apple cider. There are hand hewn wooden beams in the ceiling that date back to the mid-19th century. We keep it locked, so don't even think about sneaking down there after dark to take photos or to try to catch evidence of our ghostly prisoner who is still held captive in its depths. Later I will tell you what he did to me, but I'm not ready yet.

Climbing back up the stairs and into the sweet smelling Virginian sunlight is always rather a relief. Continuing our tour outside and to the back of the house, you can still see the evidence of two of the old porches. The brick is stained and there are holes where the porches were once attached. The small garden is meticulously kept by our grounds crew. I love walking through these gardens when I can escape from my desk. They are filled with flowers, groomed hedges and wisteria dripping down the pergola. The sidewalks in the gardens crunch when you walk on them and when you look down you can see oyster shells under your shoes. The shells were dredged from the nearby James River and were commonly used to pave roads in Williamsburg during the eighteenth century.

If we keep walking around to the left of the house we can see a gazebo sitting nearby. We rent it out for weddings and such. It was built in the 1980s. Around this Gazebo is where one of the lost graveyards used to be. Eliza's tomb stone squats back here alone in the shadows of some great oak trees. There have been many ghost sightings in this area as well.

Walking back to the front door we may have to avoid stepping in goose poo. The geese have invaded our resort in masses. They are as mean as little pterodactyls too, so please don't encourage your kids to give them a warm hug and kiss. They bite.

The back yard gardens in spring, Emily Christoff Flowers, 2011.

When we open the front door to the house we are hit with a blast of cold air and a musty smell. I can't imagine living without air conditioning in the south, how in the world did they survive? The poor inhabitants before air conditioning could have opened all of the windows to get a nice breeze, since all forty windows are symmetrical and facing each other, so maybe it wasn't so bad. The windows are tall, and the hand crafted glass was recently installed. Iris made many of the curtains and floral decorations that you see tastefully gracing the rooms. The furniture is primarily antique reproduction and was purchased from England in 1984. The house has no original furnishings.

The wooden floors were installed in 1984, but were taken from homes as old as our house. For that reason you will see that the nails are all handmade. The stairs leading up to the second floor were built after the great fire of 1842. We do not know what the original stairs looked like since the house plans were destroyed in this fire.

The large portrait hanging in the front hall is of some mystery man. We have no idea who he is, and the work is not signed. It came from England and is masterfully painted. I have named him Fred. Fred's eyes follow you as you walk through the room. This is not paranormal, but it does tend to freak out the kids.

The first and second floor rooms were originally symmetrical from the left to the right, as was customary for colonial Georgian construction. The great hall is in the center and on each side of it are 2 rooms. Each room had a fireplace set at an angle in the corner. I read that corner fireplaces were common in the architect's earlier works but in his later homes he always centered them. Mr. Taliaferro would have set these bottom floor rooms up as parlors, smoking rooms, a dining room and perhaps a music room.

You would be surprised at how many visitors are fascinated by the five modern bathrooms that they find throughout the house. The bathrooms and electricity were not installed until the mid-twentieth century. The shape of the interior rooms of the house is different now to accommodate the restrooms, and so the rooms are no longer symmetrical. It is actually quite entertaining to sit back quietly and listen to folks exclaim about how amazing it was that they had flushable toilets back then. I always do correct them after I am done laughing, and explain that they used "privies" back then, and did not even have toilet paper. Ah, my job is so much fun!

The second floor of the house is shaped exactly as the first floor. The sagging wood floors up there are not quite as old, they were installed in 1843. This is where they would have had their bedrooms, but we set them all up as community rooms. Again, I get quite a few questions about the oddity of having no bedrooms. Guests often ask if the colonists slept in the house. Once, someone even asked if they slept at all. Really, they ask this kind of thing all the time. I couldn't make this stuff up!

The stairs leading up to the third floor were also built in 1843. It was just attic space until it was set up as a modern apartment in 1984. We are certain about this since the attic contains no fireplace. Contrary to what people tend to think, it was not used to house servants and we did not chain any crazy people up there. I must admit however that I have considered it a few times.

The third floor studio now has two working showers, a modern kitchen with a microwave and refrigerator. Before you ask, let me just say that Richard Taliaferro did not have a microwave in his attic and I guarantee that he did not shower.

The Ghost of the Strict Man

The man who built this incredible mansion was a very interesting person, and I suspect that he is still sulking about his house. Besides being a master architect, he was also a master farmer. He developed an apple orchard that produced the most wonderful hard cider. This cider was so amazing that his son-in-law's best friend and student, Thomas Jefferson, took clippings of his apple tree to his own home at Monticello, and started his own orchard. This apple was named the Taliaferro apple, but unfortunately it is now extinct. Taliaferro also bred horses, was the sheriff of Williamsburg, a Justice of the Peace, a Major in the local militia, and ran a very successful large farm.

The great architect has been described as a somber and pious person. His manner was almost grave and his humor rarely light hearted. He was a strict master, but just and compassionate. His job as Sherriff in 1741 was to execute condemned men, summonsing and impaneling jury, making arrests, ducking, whipping or imprisoning criminals and serving summons. Accounts of his later years describe a reclusive man who shunned social gatherings and preferred the isolation of his country home. He sounds like a whole lot of fun, doesn't he? I bet he was the life of the party. (Lanciano, 130)

I have no doubt that Richard Taliaferro was a firm master of his family and his business, and so I have often pondered if he could be the ghost that we call "The Strict Man", or "The Master". When guests describe the specter of the strict man it is almost as if they are quoting the personality of Taliaferro directly from his biographer. I find this observation very interesting since I did not come across the biography of Taliaferro until 2012, but witnesses have been describing this ghost since the mid-1980s.

According to witnesses, they describe a male authoritative ghost standing protectively by the front door, who is trying to shoo visitors away. They don't feel that he is evil, just angry and very strict. We also have heard countless stories about people getting locked out of the house, being locked in the rooms inside of the house, or being told to "GET OUT!" He especially despises rude children. This is a fun thing to say on the tours, as the kids usually behave really well for me for the rest of the hour after they hear this. I'm so bad.

In 2010 one psychic told me that our Strict Man used to be the master of the plantation and he feels that his home should not be a show place for all of these visitors. He is offended by our coarse manners and wishes for us to leave. He doesn't mind me or most of my coworkers because he sees us often and we are respectful, but he is leery of strangers, especially the vulgar ones.

Could this be the reason why I felt very anxious the first time that I entered the house, but after a while I felt safe when I walked through the front doors? Many other coworkers or guests cannot bring themselves to even walk past the main entrance. Maybe it is because the famous architect never left his beloved farm, and he doesn't like people. He just wants all of these silly people to get out of his home and stay out!

My first personal experience with the master came at a surprise to me. I was sitting at my easel out at the gazebo near the front door, just a few weeks after starting my new job. It was a beautiful fall southern day in 2006. The sky was vibrant blue, and all of the leaves had turned a crisp orange, yet the air was still warm and moist. It was too perfect to sit in the dark front room, so I lugged my easel and chalks outside. At one point I noticed a family struggling to open the front door. It sometimes sticks, so I walked back and attempted to open it for them, but it was locked. I was stumped. You have to use a key to lock it and no one had done so.

Now remember, I was not permitted to literally tell the guests that the house was haunted, but Belinda never said that I couldn't talk to the ghosts in front of the guests. I took a step back, and shouted up to the second floor, "You better come down here and open this door and stop scaring these poor people. If you don't unlock it right this minute I am going to call the curator and she is going to be mad!" You see, most people were a little scared of Belinda, myself included. I shook my finger at the house just so the ghost knew that I meant business.

I tried the door again, and it swung right open. The family was stunned. They asked me if the house was haunted, and I just shrugged my shoulders. I had my poker face perfected by then.

A few weeks later I was sitting outside at my easel again when this young lady came in to work her shift. Anna was a high school student who taught some sewing classes after school. She was scared to death of the ghosts, but my co-worker Jon still loved to jump out of dark corners and scream "BOO!" in the poor girl's face. Thanks to his cruel wit she was very nervous in the house as you can imagine.

She waved happily to me as she walked past, but when she got to the door it was locked. As before, I tried to open it and sure enough it would not budge. I took a step back, shouted up to the second floor, "You better stop teasing Anna. She is going to be late for work. Please open the door!" The door swung open. She refused to enter the house alone, so I walked with her up to the top floor, and assured her that everything would be ok. Of course Jon teased her relentlessly about this for the next several weeks.

In the winter of 2007 we had a guest artist by the name of Dina set up once a week in the music room doing a pearl demonstration. I was not permitted to tell her about the ghosts so I hoped that they would leave her alone and not try to tease her or scare her away.

My worst fears were realized when Dina confronted me to ask why she had been locked out of the back hallway where she had her equipment stored. She was a bit miffed. I knew that the master was messing with her because the music room door does not have a lock on it. I walked over to the door and attempted to open it, hoping that it was just swollen shut, but to my amazement I could not budge the door knob. It was as if someone was firmly holding it from the back hallway.

I told the artist that I would go and find a key. I really hate lying about the ghosts, but my boss said I had to, so I did.

Shaking my head and frowning to myself I walked through the house around to the other side of the door where the invisible hands were holding it tight. I whispered softly, "Please stop teasing Dina and open the door?" I waited a moment then tried the door again and it opened right up. Dina just thanked me for unlocking it. I tried to keep a straight face as I responded, "You are welcome."

If you have ever visited Colonial Williamsburg during the Christmas season you will be very surprised to hear that citizens of the capital did not actually decorate their houses for Christmas in the 18th century. There is no way that early Americans would have wasted fresh fruit to hang on their doors. The Williamsburg style of decorating for the holidays actually originated in 1936, in hopes of luring more people to visit the museum. It worked. (Oliver)

Even though the architect who built the manor house would not have decorated his home for Christmas, Iris always has it decked out beautifully for the holidays, for the enjoyment of today's modern tourists. She tends to lean towards the Victorian era of decorating combined with the "Williamsburg style", and the house is simply breathtaking under her artistic eye. She spends many hours preparing, and often works long into the night the first few weeks of December.

Front foyer at Christmas time, Emily Christoff Flowers, 2009

One night Iris was preparing for the holidays up in the studio. It was past midnight and she was exhausted. She was making wreaths for the Christmas party, and was bound and determined to get them done before she left for the day. She was startled when she heard a deep voice come from the corner of the room. It said, "Get out". She searched the room but there was no one there so she went back to work, blaming the incident on her tired mind.

The strict man didn't give up easily, so again he told her to, "get out!" She ignored him once more, hoping that he would go away.

The third time he said, "GET OUT!" Iris stood up, put her hands on her hip and said, "Dude, I got way too much work to do and I am not leaving until I am done!"

When Iris gets mad her face tends to get very red, and she gets quite worked up. I am sure that she put the ghost in his place. She went back to work, and he left her alone for the rest of the night, most likely sulking in his corner. He should have known better than to cross Iris while she is crafting, even I wouldn't do that.

I was teaching a guest service class to my co-workers on the third floor one time in 2009, when the Strict Man apparently decided to join in on the lesson. The focus of this week's class was about how to communicate with good manners, and the importance of not interrupting guests. What was really irritating was that throughout the class this young lady kept interrupting me, wanting to know more about the ghosts instead of focusing on our lesson. This girl was really getting on my last nerve because she would not stop whispering to her neighbor, rolling her eyes at me and changing the subject back to ghosts. When the class was finally over she exclaimed that she was going to catch herself a ghost, and she started taunting the spirits and making fun of me in front of the class. I planned on tattling on her the next time I saw Iris.

She bounced excitedly out of the room and down the stairs to the second floor bathroom. Charles, a security guard, knew this rambunctious girl and thought that he better follow her to make sure that she wouldn't harm herself or get into any trouble.

He stood next to her as she reached for the bathroom door handle. Just as she was about to grab the open door, it slammed hard right in her face, as if it was pushed forcefully from behind. I could feel the entire house tremor from the impact all the way up to the third floor. Her scream echoed through the rooms.

She stood paralyzed with shock as Charles slowly opened the door, but much to his amazement the room was empty. He swore that she did not shut it herself, and I believe him. The girl ran back to the stairs and shouted up to me that she had found herself a ghost. Her face was white as a sheet; she was fighting back tears and trembling. Charles was nodding his head, and also looked a bit amazed.

The bathroom and office on the second floor
Notice the orbs in the photo.
Emily Christoff Flowers, 2010

I remembered that only a moment before she was making fun of me for seeing ghosts. Who could resist a snarky answer? I casually said "Oh that's nice, glad to see that you finally met one." I smiled down the stairs at her as pleasantly as I could.

I guess she didn't like my response and so she ran screaming out of the house, and was upset for the entire rest of the day. Fortunately for me, she never returned to the house. I have thanked the strict man for that many times since then.

The Master made another attempt to relieve the house of rude visitors a year later in July of 2010. Late at night, after completing a very long and hot ghost tour, a mother with three teen age girls approached me and demanded that I give them a private tour, since they missed the first one. I am in the hospitality industry, and I am not allowed to say no, and so I kept my opinion to myself and smiled. I gave them permission to walk through the house until security locked it up, but I was a bit irked at their attitude with me. I think that our strict man had a pretty good idea how I felt, and made it clear that he shared my opinion

As I was cleaning up in the dining room, the family walked up to the third floor. I heard the three girls scream at the top of their lungs. They raced down both flights of stairs with their ponytails flying behind them, and didn't stop until they came to the front door. I heard them hesitate then squeal again and run out of the house, slamming the door behind them. They yowled all the way back to their unit.

I asked their mother if they were alright, and she just shook her head, puzzled. She had no idea what happened, and just apologized for their behavior. Being the mother of a teen age girl myself I felt a bit of sympathy for her, and gave her my card. I told her that if they e-mailed me that I would send a few stories to them. When I got home I checked my e-mail and had already received a letter from the girls explaining their behavior.

The e-mail explained that as they were in the third floor studio they heard a man's deep voice say, "GET OUT!" Their mother did not hear it. The girls ran screaming down the stairs but by the time they got to the front door they had calmed down. As they hesitated, considering going back up the stairs again, all three heard the man's angry voice again say "GET OUT", this time right in their ear.

They shot out of the house, never to return. I found their story very compelling since they had no knowledge of this ghost before this unfortunate encounter. It feels pretty good having the Strict Man on my side.

The Prisoner in the Basement

It has been speculated more than once that perhaps some bad citizen of Williamsburg was held prisoner in the basement by Sherriff Taliaferro. I think that he is still there in spirit, and is not very happy about it. Others speculate that this angry entity is a former slave, an angry Native American or perhaps a captive from one of the wars hiding in the depths of the house. The origins of this ghost are pure speculation, but there is no doubt that there is something bad down there.

One security guard told me that a guest claimed to have been attacked while in the basement. He said that this man came up to him and asked if he would please confirm to his girlfriend that the Manor House really was haunted. Apparently she didn't believe her boyfriend when he told her that a brick popped out of the cellar wall, shot across the room in front of his face and nearly hit him in the nose. The man was quite shaken up and was upset with her for calling him a liar. He hoped that having a security guard to back him up would provoke an apology from her, but the faithful employee just shook his head. He was forbidden to share our dirty little secret at that time. I felt a little sorry for the man having to deal with his teasing girlfriend when they got home. I knew how he felt.

One of our IT techs has worked here for over 20 years, so I figured that if anyone had seen anything down there it would be this man. David told me that many years ago, as he was working in the maintenance department, he and another employee needed to go into the basement to do some kind of repair work. The other employee walked in first and got all the way into the back room when he screamed and ran out as fast as he could. David watched him run all the way past the tennis courts, screeching for his life. He never came back. The man stubbornly refused to tell anyone what he saw, and for the rest of the many years that he worked here he would not return to the basement. He always managed to send someone else to do those jobs for him and he would not come near the house ever again.

A few years later David was in the basement alone working on some phone lines. He walked past the first room and noticed that there was a table in the corner with a whole bunch of pots and pans, piled on top of a metal tray. When he walked into the back room something or someone knocked off all of that stuff and it made a huge crash. He immediately zipped right back in there but he didn't see anything or anyone that might have done that. David's bright blue eyes sparkled as he told me this story, and explained that it was freaky, but really kind of cool. He says that he is not a type of person to believe in ghosts, but he believes every story that people say about the house.

When I first started giving the tours the resort allowed me bring guests down to experience the basement for themselves. After a while I became sure that the rumors were true, that there was something evil watching us from its gloomy depths. By the end of the third month of tours I could not even bring myself to go down past the bottom step. I felt as if there was someone hiding in the shadows, glaring at me with hatred. I often became sick to my stomach and found it difficult to breathe.

I had only once before felt such a vile sensation of being watched with hate from a distance like that. I once went to a middle school dance, where I wore my older sister's hand me down lavender prom dress. I was sporting my Farrah Fawcett hairdo, and wearing an overabundance of ice blue eye shadow. I could feel all of those insufferable eyes on me. Yes my friend, the feelings of hatred in the basement is just as horrific as attending a 7th grade dance.

On many tours the guests experienced the same sensations of hate regardless of the fact that I did not express my fear to them. Batteries also often became drained, cameras stopped working, and sometimes people got pinched. One person said that something jumped onto her back. Other guests have taken photos showing mists or shadows in the shape of a man's face.

I have had several psychics visit the tours. What is interesting is that all of them seem to say the exact same things about this bad entity without prior consultation. They said that there is a dead man hiding down there who hates me personally. They described him as having beady black piercing eyes, dark skin, and a wound. He was being held prisoner for something that he did which was very bad. He hides down there because people rarely go down into the cellar, and he prefers his isolation. He despises me because I was the first person to allow strangers into the basement, and to talk openly about ghosts.

After the third psychic told me this I only went into the basement one more time. My experience caused nightmares for months. I was very relieved when I was eventually informed by the resort's safety coordinator that they deemed the basement unsafe to bring guests into due to the uneven floors and clutter filling the rooms. I am sure the prisoner was delighted as well when I stopped visiting him.

There is an orb in this photo. Can you also see the glow coming from one of the windows? Photo by Shelley Thacker Millirons, 2008

Chapter Four

The Birth of Our Country

The property went through some changes during the late 18th century. Richard Taliaferro died of "Gout of the head" in 1779. Taliaferro's daughter, Elizabeth, married George Wythe, who was a signer of the Declaration of Independence, as well as the first law professor in the United States. Elizabeth and George Wythe were loaned Taliaferro's townhouse in Williamsburg, which we now call the Wythe House. (Lanciano,184) The Wythe house is the identical twin of our own Manor House and is said to be one of the most haunted homes in Williamsburg, but that's another long ghost story.

George and Elizabeth often fostered intelligent young men who had promising futures. Counted among his greatest protégés were such leading intellects as Henry Clay, James Monroe and John Marshall. Wythe's prize pupil was the great President Thomas Jefferson, who recognized his "faithful and beloved mentor" as having made him "the honest advocate of my country's rights." (Chadwick)

Strange Little Footsteps

I heard a peculiar bit of gossip about Wythe's sad murder that sort of ties in with our manor house ghosts. In 1806, when Wythe was in his later years, he took in a young boy named Michael Brown as his foster child and pupil. Michael's mother was a slave, and his father was a white man. Michael was Wythe's most recent intellectual apprentice, and was greatly loved by the elderly judge. He had wonderful plans for Michael and expected him to be a great leader someday.

When Wythe's greedy nephew, George Wythe Sweeny, discovered that the son of a slave was an heir to a large part of his uncle's immense estate, he poisoned the judge, the boy and his uncle's faithful servant, Lydia Broadnax. Obviously the scoundrel expected to get most of the inheritance if he wiped out the entire household.

Poor Michael and his great teacher died, but Lydia lived. Although she witnessed Sweeny put poison the coffee pot, her testimony, and additional witness from several other slaves, were prohibited in court, since blacks, free or slave, were prohibited from testifying against whites in a court of law. Even second-hand testimony from blacks was inadmissible. Wythe and Jefferson had considered changing this law several years prior, but were unsuccessful. The great judge's death took 14 agonizing and heartbreaking days. During this time he disinherited Sweeny, however this corrupt young man walked free. (Chadwick)

I found this tragedy compelling, since Wythe was family of Taliaferro. I was hungry for more information. I was quite startled when I read a little blurb in Taliaferro's biography which gave an explanation of George's love for Michael, and could explain some of our ghosts here on this property.

According to the biographer, the rumor is that Michael Brown was the son of Richard Taliaferro Sr. and his cook, making him Elizabeth Wythe's brother. (Lanciano, 184) The math doesn't quite add up, so perhaps he could have been the son of Richard Jr. But in either case, if he was the son of a Taliaferro, most likely Michael was born and raised by his slave mother at the Taliaferro plantation before moving in with Judge Wythe. He would have had an emotional connection to what was his home just a short time before his tragic and sudden death.

Taliaferro's legitimate son, Richard Jr., served as a colonel in the American Revolution. He married Rebecca Cocke of Surry County, and lived with her in the manor house with their ten children. I have located the names of the first eight. They are, Anne, Benjamin, Elizabeth, Lucy, Rebecca, Richard, Sarah and Robert. These kids were the same age as young Michael Brown, and so they may have played together in the yard and around the plantation. Could poor young Michael's innocent spirit still reside at his place of birth near where his mother worked in the Kitchen? It could explain some of the ghostly sounds of children's footsteps which are often heard in that building, in the units, and in the General store.

This home was built by Taliaferro and given to his daughter and her husband, George Wythe. It is the twin to our manor house.
Emily Christoff Flowers 2012

Revolutionary War at the Farm

The city of Williamsburg did not experience a tremendous amount of bloodshed during the Revolutionary war, but it did have a skirmish called the battle of Green Spring, about a mile away from the Taliaferro home. General Cornwallis hid his British troops in the swampy forests behind our plantation before attacking Anthony Wayne and his rebel Americans, who were camped at the Green Spring farm. Various descriptions of this battle explain that although the Green Spring home was used for the camp, most of the actual fighting occurred on the property of "a neighboring farm". We were that neighboring farm.

130 American rebels and 75 British soldiers lost their lives in and around our plantation. After this confrontation in our back yard Cornwallis marched his troops to Yorktown where he was held in siege by General George Washington, and surrendered his English Troops. America had finally won her freedom.

Ghost Lady of the Woods

There is a female ghost that we associate with the Revolutionary era. Several times a year, for the past several decades, our guests call security at odd hours of the night to report that they see a desolate woman with very long flowing brunette hair. She is wandering hopelessly around the dark swamp behind the resort. People often see her out of the corner of their eye, but when they look again she has vanished. She wears a glowing white dress which looks like a nightgown or a colonial style shift, and is usually seen in the woods behind buildings 28,29, and 30 and also units 44 through 47.

I chose to paint the lady of the woods for the front cover of this book by the way, because I find her so fascinating. I also thought that my 17 year old daughter, Halee, would make an excellent model for her since she often wonders hopelessly around her dark swamp of a bedroom searching for lost socks.

In case you were wondering, I did the painting on my computer using a digital tablet and Photoshop, isn't that cool? It is odd not getting paint under my nails, in my hair and up my nose. I rather like it.

You can also see that Halee was very upset with mom for making her pose yet again, as this shot was taken right after the eye roll, hair flip thing that all teenage girls have perfected. I paint her a lot, much to her dismay.

Anyhow, as I was saying, our mysterious lady seems to be distraught and frantically searching for something, or someone in the woods and in the gardens behind the house. What makes this ghost story so astounding is that these reports come from guests visiting from all over the world, who give the same exact descriptions of this poor unfortunate wraith. The witnesses do not know each other, have not read any other accounts of our ghost, and often mistake her for a lost human. Until now, no one has associated her with the ghost of Jamestown. People had often connected her with the time of the Revolutionary War, due to her style of dress.

A recent increase in sightings in the winter of 2012 spiked my curiosity and so I began searching for any clue to who this woman might be. I was thrilled when I read the book, "The Ghosts of Williamsburg, Volume II", written by L.B.Taylor, which seemed to describe the exact same ghost. They call her Lydia Ambler.

The wealthy Lydia allegedly fell in love with a soldier named Alexander Maupin. They married in August of 1776, and then he left soon after to fight for American independence. He never came back to his poor Lydia. Folk lore states that the young socialite waited for her love to return to her, often standing on the shores of the James River, or wondering through the woods in hopes of seeing him come home. Finally, after assuming that he married her only for her money, and then abandoned her, she took her own life in a fit of rage. Her apparition has been seen many times since the time of her death throughout the woods and on the shores of the Jamestown Island.

Employees of the National park service have described her exactly as our witnesses describe our own ghost. They see her as an angry woman, wearing a gown of the revolutionary period, roaming the grounds as if searching for Alexander. They know that she is not an employee, reenacting in a costume, since she vanishes right in front of their eyes. Could this ghost be our same mysterious lady of the woods?

I began searching for some sort of connection between Lydia and our Lady of the Woods, since the sightings were so similar, and only a few miles from each other. I wasn't able to find much information about Lydia herself, but I did discover that the carcass of her family's lavish brick home still stands in the Jamestown National Park. This is where she is often seen by Jamestown employees.

I discovered that the Ambler Mansion was built around 1750, which was the same time that Taliaferro was living in the Manor house, and at the height of his architectural career. It was burned during the Revolutionary and Civil Wars, and was restored after both. When it burned again in 1895, it wasn't rebuilt. There is a sign next to the ruins which describe it as looking identical to the Wythe House, which still stands in Colonial Williamsburg.

This had to be the connection! Our Manor house is referred to as the twin to the Wythe House, and both were built by the same man.

I found a photo of the Ambler house right before it was destroyed for the final time. I clutched the monitor as I realized that it was totally identical to our Manor House. Could Lydia's spirit be drawn to our house because it reminds her of her own home? Could this poor girl have visited the Taliaferro farm while she was in grief? She was the same age and social status as the Taliaferro children, so this is very possible. So far I have not been successful in finding out who built the Ambler Mansion, but of course I consider that it might have been Taliaferro, since it is identical to his other homes and built at the same time. (Cotton)

The coincidence between the two entities is amazing. I now believe that we have a name for our lady of the woods. The poor lost soul's name is Lydia Ambler.

The Spirits of Slaves

Pocahontas's husband, John Rolfe, cultivated a very sweet tobacco which he brought to the new world from Trinidad. Jamestown became successful after it was discovered that this tobacco was a profitable export. Most farmers in this area grew this crop, and Taliaferro family was no exception. With the farming of tobacco however came the increasing popularity of purchasing African slaves to work in the fields.

I honestly did not know that Jamestown was the first port to accept African slaves in the new colonies until my recent studies. When I found this out I was very surprised and sad. These first African slaves were from Angola, were captured during a war with the Portuguese and brought to Jamestown in 1619, most likely as indentured servants. Indentured servants are usually free after about seven years of service to their masters, and given land and a few other material possessions. A slave is usually a slave for life until they are able to purchase their freedom. At first the slaves that were brought to the new world were from many different countries and races. Unfortunately, over the course of the next century, the slavery system in the south became race-based. By the beginning of the new century a majority of African Americans were slaves for life.

According to Taliaferro's last will and testament, he had 20 slaves that worked the farm for him at the time of his death. Some of these slaves may have been the ancestors of the first slaves from Angola, but at least 2 are thought to have been born in Africa. The slave quarters were set apart from the manor house and would have been similar to a small village, with their own gardens and small one room homes. Artifacts from these small stone and wood huts have been located in the woods behind the kitchen. No other evidence or foundations of these quarters remain.

According to old newspaper articles, there were about 100 slaves living on this farm at the time that the Union troupes burned the manor house and slave quarters in 1842. It's no surprise that many visitors over the years see what they believe are the ghosts of these unfortunate people. (Virginia Gazette, 1942)

Manor House and Kitchen, Emily Christoff Flowers 2008

One of the most commonly seen ghosts is described as a friendly older black man, perhaps once a house servant or slave, who is dressed in black period clothing and likes to flirt with the ladies. We fondly refer to him as "Gus", but we do not know what his true name was

Melanie started working at the resort in 1986, only two years after they started building the resort around the house. All of the offices were inside of the manor house at that time, and her desk was on the second floor. She told me that she never felt alone, but she also never felt threatened. Many times she would be sitting in her office and feel her pretty long blonde hair being blown by a random gust of wind, like fingers on her neck. She would look out the window, but there would be no breeze. She always figured it was a ghost playing with her hair. That's why she named this friendly flirt, "Gus". She and her coworkers thought the name seemed to fit a sweet old guy who would watch over them, and tease them playfully.

The most amazing thing happened to Melanie in late October of 1987. It was after dusk and she had gone to the security gate at the end of the main road to clock out, after locking the house up for the night. She was chatting with the security guard when she glanced back and saw someone standing in front of the middle window. Melanie's first panicked thought was that she had accidentally locked a guest in the house and they were unable to get out. She frantically ran as fast as she could back to the front door and keyed herself back in. She checked the entire house, top to bottom, and it was empty.

Melanie was very excited when she realized that she finally saw an image of Gus for herself. To this day, Melanie is very proud to have had one of the first documented ghost sightings at the resort.

I have heard many other rumors over the years of people glancing into the windows of the house after it was locked for the night, and seeing a handsome older black man smiling back at them. This same man also seems to fit the description of a man sometimes seen walking around the property.

Iris was driving home one evening after dark in 2006, when she passed a man walking along the side of the road near the security gate. She was startled because she almost hit him.

He was hard to see in the gloom since he was wearing all black clothing and a black hat. It seemed almost as if he was in mourning clothes. He also had very dark black skin and a grey beard. She was rather flustered about almost hitting him, so she glanced in her rearview mirror immediately after passing him, but he had vanished into thin air. There was no place for him to hide, and so she realized that she had just witnessed the man Melanie named Gus.

Iris also told me that a maintenance man saw an older, dark skinned man dressed in odd looking black clothing, standing in one of the units, and gazing out at him through the second floor bathroom window. This alarmed the employee since the unit was listed as unoccupied, so he entered the apartment and searched around for an intruder. He walked into the hot tub room and the door violently slammed behind him so hard that he thought it had broken the glass. Undaunted, he continued searching the unit, including the second floor, but found it to be totally empty. When he got back into his truck and pulled out of the parking lot the old guy was in the window again, staring at him from under a black hat.

Many years later Gus will thoroughly enjoy our ghost tours, especially the attention of the ladies who attended. It seems that Gus is quite the tease! There have been at least 5 separate tours in which female guests would claim that they could feel an invisible man's hand gently pat their leg or back side, only to turn around and see that they were standing alone. Once, an older female guest came up to me after a tour, blushing and giggling excitedly. She claimed that playful Gus had just patted her bottom. It made her day. In fact, judging by the sparkle in her eye and her husband's stormy expression, I would bet that it was the highlight of her entire vacation!

Civil War in Jamestown, Library of Congress, C 1862. This photo was taken about 4 miles from the Manor House.

Chapter Five

Phantoms of the Civil War

After Colonel Richard Taliaferro Jr.'s death, his widow, Rebecca, continued to successfully run the plantation herself. After her death in 1810, The 1,075 acre plantation was purchased by Richard Hannon of Petersburg, who had married one of Rebecca's granddaughters. Mr. Hannon farmed the plantation for a few years but by 1819 he had sold it to Pleasant Akin of Petersburg, who in turn conveyed it to Shadrack Alfriend of Amelia County. At this time the farm was handed over to tenant farmers, who allowed it to fall into deep disrepair, before being purchased by Thomas Martin in 1827. Thomas's son, Dr. William Martin owned in the farm where our story now picks up. (Lanciano, pg 97)

Walking in the Shoes of a Confederate

Although I have lived in Williamsburg for over 20 years, I had no idea that there was so much bloodshed in our little resort town during the Civil War. Before I started researching for the tours I thought of our town as just a tourist destination, with lots of waffle houses, a rather commercialized living museum, and a huge amusement park. It is not uncommon to see flocks of children stomping around town wearing their plastic tri-cornered hats and blowing on those darn screechy penny whistles. They would be very surprised to hear how devastated Williamsburg was when the Yankees swept through. What I was soon to learn was nothing short of fantastic.

Are you ready for another history lesson? Oh stop rolling your eyes, I will keep it quick. Besides, I think you will find this very interesting, especially since it seems to be the cause of so many of our ghost sightings in and around the house.

As I have mentioned before, history is not my forte, however, after reading several particularly descriptive journals about the civil war in Williamsburg, I was able to paint a vivid picture in my mind of how it might have looked to the eyes of the poor citizens of our little burg. You can tell I am really getting into the history now, and that I don't hate it anymore.

If you and I were to stroll arm and arm down the main street of Duke of Gloucester, a year after Virginia succeeded on April of 1861, we would see a town filled with sick and injured men. All the exhausted confederate soldiers in the area have flocked here, you see. Most of them are not hurt from gunshot, but are suffering from disease or malnutrition. They are hungry, thin, tattered, and pale.

If they are injured from gunshot, and unfortunate enough to have a bullet suck in their arm or leg, the overwhelmed surgeons will have to cut the limb off.

Did you know that these doctors didn't wash their hands between surgeries? They wore blood and pus stained coats, and they didn't even rinse off their saw most of the time. Heck, for all we know they might even have wiped their tools on a bootstrap with horse muck stuck to it. They were not negligent; they just don't know any better at that time (Adams)

Anyhow, as we move towards the buildings used as hospitals, we catch a glimpse of a pile of decapitated arms and legs stewing in the mid-day heat. They are hidden under a cloud of flies beneath the open windows, where the fatigued doctors flung them out after each speedy operation. The soldiers usually have nothing to numb the pain either while they are doing this, but losing a leg or two will save their life. You see, there is no way to fight infection during this time unfortunately. (John)

Yorktown, Virginia. Confederate battery. Magruder with 8-inch Columbaids. Federal transports in river. Library of Congress, 1862

If the soldiers are lucky they might get a swig of liquor before their surgery, or perhaps a bit of opium to dull the pain. After getting their wounds packed with unsterilized lint, and sobering up, they usually walk or are carried to a nearby plantation, school or church to recover. While there they might get small doses of whiskey or quinine to help with the recovery. I am pretty sure that many of these poor sick men were brought to the manor house to recover or perhaps in some cases to die in the arms of Dr. Martin and his family.

As we walk through the stench of the muddy Main Street, we see that most of the grand buildings have been abandoned and ransacked. Many of the families have set up camp out in the woods to flee Union bullets. Most slaves ran for their freedom to the city of Hampton already. Some of the elderly or very faithful slaves have not yet left.

A few adventurous families stayed in town to protect their property. They don't want to venture out into the daylight however. Most just peer silently at us from the security of their homes, through closed blinds, indignant at the defilement of their city.

The balmy May breeze has carried with it the scent of gore mingled with the soft scent of honeysuckle. The butter cups that filled the Palace Green seem to mock the thousands of wounded who fill every open space. We heard rumor that almost 4000 men have died in Williamsburg, but there looks to be many more than that filling the blood soaked earth. I don't blame the poor citizens of this once grand town for staying hidden away indoors.

As we pass the cruciform shaped structure of the old Bruton Parish, we can hear soft moaning. Following the cries of the injured takes us into the ancient cemetery, and we see poorly clad soldiers, laying in shock, on and between the white grave slabs. Blood is splattered on the tombs, where death met men who were placed in the shadows of the tall magnolia trees to die. Some have yet to be removed and lowered into their hastily dug graves.

The inside of the church is destroyed. The pews, in which many of our countries greatest leaders once sat, including George Washington, Thomas Jefferson and Patrick Henry, are torn up and the cushions ripped to shreds. Cots and stretchers, occupied by dying rebels fill every space in the once lavish house of worship. Their lifeblood covers the floor, and it sticks to bottom of our shoes. (Bruton Parish)

58

Civil War Drum Corps, Library of Congress, C1862

The distant sound of music overpowers the cries of the dying, and we quickly walk back out into the blinding sun to see what the commotion is all about. Marching bands of musicians mock our grief with songs of victory, such as Yankee Doodle, Dixie and John Brown's Body. A line of enemy artillery marches in step, led by freshly caparisoned horses, dressed as if no carnage had occurred just the day before. Twenty eight bands of regiment followed them, as the few shocked people who wander the streets turn their backs on them. How could they murder our boys and then march down our streets in celebration? I gather my blood stained skirts and we shrink away in disgust. (Hudson)

Death in Williamsburg

I bet you are wondering what happened to provoke all of this grief. See, what actually transpired is much more interesting than what I read in my dry history book back in High School. I still think that the only thing that book was good for was for bonking my little brothers on their heads when they irritated me. In fact, I doubt that I read much of it since I barely passed the class. Now that I have done some more reading, I understand much better what happened. I am going to explain it to you the way that I wish it had been explained to me.

The Peninsular Campaign was said to be the single most ambitious Union operation of the American Civil war. In 1862, an army of over 41,000 Union soldiers were transported by sea to Fort Monroe, to the east of the Confederate capitol of Richmond. The Federal Army, led by General George B. McClellan, hoped to sneak up on Richmond's back door without having to face an entrenched opponent. This meant that his men would tramp through our little town on the way to Richmond. By destroying the capital of the confederacy, he hoped to put an early end to the bloody Civil War, but he and his men were about to get a big surprise in Williamsburg. (Williams)

A small but fierce group of Confederate defenders were waiting for them on Old Williamsburg Road. Colonel John B. Magruder occupied 15 entrenched redoubts, and successfully slowed the advance of the Union Troops as they marched through the quiet city of Williamsburg. This two day battle eventually gave the south extra time to protect Richmond, prolonging the end of the war by several years. Estimated casualties in Williamsburg were 3,843 total (US 2,283; CS 1,560) (Rickard)

Ft. Magruder and the other redoubts were located on the same road that led right past our manor house back then. Locals described skirmishes fought on the swamp land surrounding his house during this retreat. Maps show troops passing through the fields and roads in front of us, and it is commonly believed that the manor house was used as a hospital during this time, especially since it was owned by a medical doctor. I have tried for many years to find a record that it was used for this purpose, but the only information that I have uncovered so far was that most large private buildings, like the poor Bruton Parish and surrounding plantation homes, became full of the injured or dead.

Morbid Apparitions of War

Ghost sightings of this time period are actually pretty frequent. No shock there, huh? Some people have seen visions of spectral piles of men dead and in the process of dying, stacked up along the walls of the basement. This was pretty common practice during war I guess. There were never enough doctors to save everyone, so they would separate the ones they could treat from the ones they couldn't. The poor men who were in very bad shape were stacked with the dead. The basement is much cooler than the house, so it would have made an excellent temporary morgue. They would have been buried pretty quick.

In April of 2012, just before I was about to whisk this little book off to the publisher, I had a very lovely visit from my good friend Lucy, who is a very talented professional psychic. You will hear some amazing stories about Lucy later, but I wanted to mention what she saw in the back yard of the manor house.

Although the house was closed to the public for renovation at the time of her visit, Matt gave us a private tour through the house. When Lucy was in the house she said that the female presence in the home was very confused. She told Lucy that she was "perturbed" at all of these men in her house banging around. She asked me to go in and talk to Eliza and explain to her what was going on. I wonder how I am going to do that without confusing the small army of construction workers trudging in and out of the house

Since my most recent studies uncovered the evidence of a second graveyard, I asked Lucy to accompany me around the grounds to see how she would respond to the tennis court area. I expected Lucy to see graves from the 17th century and echoes from the Native American massacres during Bacons Rebellion. I figured that she would sense casualties of this time, buried long before the house was built, since this is what old newspaper articles suggested.

As we wandered through the manicured gardens she became almost physically ill. She sensed a graveyard, but not from burials many years ago as I had read. She sensed newer graves that were dug in haste and were left unmarked.

She said that she saw hundreds, maybe even thousands of corpses, shrouded in white cloth, lying on the ground in rows awaiting burial. She could smell their stench and see the brick house in the background. The ground was all dirt with no grass and covered in blood.

She said that the graceful beauty of our groomed resort was in horrific contrast to the violence and disease of this death scene. She believed that she just had a vision of the devastation caused by the Civil War.

Lucy and a few other psychics said that they felt that the blue room was used as an operating room. It is close to the kitchen, it is on the first floor, and it is one of the largest rooms in the house, so I found this to be believable. The most exciting experience involving a Civil War ghost occurred right in the middle of one of my tours in this very room.

The Ghost of a Wounded Soldier

Few visitors know the history of the road in front of the house, and so I was quite excited when a woman on one of my tours mentioned this important thoroughfare. She said that she had a great uncle who loved to tell the family stories about his experiences during the Civil War. She said that she didn't know where exactly his event had occurred; only that it was on an old back road in Williamsburg, called Old Williamsburg Road. She did not realize that the road in front of the house was once called Williamsburg road, but has since changed names.

The woman told us that her ancestor was shot in the face while marching down Williamsburg Road, on his way to

Richmond in 1862. It was pouring rain and the dirt road was muddy and flooded. Her uncle slowly crawled off to the side of the road and was left for dead, along with many of the other soldiers. Although he was covered in blood and close to passing out, he somehow got the strength to crawl through the mud to the closest farm, where he received medical care and survived.

Winter Camp on the James River, Library of Congress, C1862

As she was telling this story to a hushed crowd, my KII meter, which I use as a ghost detector, started flashing off and on very quickly. It wasn't just giving lame little flickers, it was quickly flashing from one level to another, and all the way up to red, as if to get my attention.

I guess I should explain to you what a KII is before I move on. A KII meter is basically an electromagnetic field detector, used to detect bursts of electric magnetic energy. The pros think that ghosts emit extra amounts of this energy, and so when a ghost is standing nearby the theory is that it causes the lights to flash. You can ask a ghost to wave his hands in front of the device to answer yes or no questions. I should note for you skeptics that it also flashes when you walk past a faulty lamp, an old air conditioner, or a poorly wired electrical outlet.

Usually I pull out this little meter for the guests to play with while we walk through the house. The kids think it's cool since it is the same kind that the Ghost Hunters on T.V. use. To be quite honest with you I always thought that KII meters were a bunch of baloney. I normally handed the meter to a kid to hold while I talk about the Civil War, just as a fun prop, with no expectations of it finding a ghost. Let me tell you, I was more shocked than the kid standing next to me with her eyes all bugged out when it started to spike during this story. I nearly dropped it.

We all sat in amazement and watched slack jawed as the guest completed her account and the KII went berserk in my hand. When she was done the KII stopped cold. The woman asked if a soldier who fought on Old Williamsburg Road was trying to communicate with us, and it started flashing again. That ghost must have been doing the Hokey Pokey and flapping his hands in front of it, since it was flashing so hard. She was moved to tears. I was left speechless, which as you can imagine happens very rarely, or at least that's what my man says.

The Apparition in a Slouch Hat

We have had many ghost sightings of Civil War soldiers in and around the property and near the tomb stone standing by the home. Diana, who works in security, told me this amazing story.

It was dark and very cold outside as she arrived for work at 6:30 am on a December morning in 2009. She was driving down the main road as usual when she noticed a man standing in the gazebo wearing a Civil War uniform. It was right before Christmas, and the gazebo had all of those icicle lights around it. She could see him very clearly, but she could only see him from chest up. He appeared to be floating, as if he was standing where the ground would be before the building was put there.

She described him as a white man, with a dark mustache, and a goatee that came to a sharp point. He wasn't wearing all of the frilly things you usually see on Confederate uniforms, but was wearing a very simple grey jacket. He had on a grey hat with an emblem on it. The brim of the hat was full and not turned up. As she drove around the curve of the drive she was looking right at him, and it looked like he was looking back at her.

Her heart skipped a beat as she lost sight of him for a brief moment, because when she looked back he was gone. She jumped out of her car and took a quick look around but she was alone in the early morning gloom. As usual all of security was called, but no one else had seen him. They could find no sign of a man dressed that way wandering around the units.

After Diana told me this remarkable story she and I got on the computer and tried to find the uniform in old photos. We found everything but the hat. It was such an odd hat, we had never heard of anyone from that era wearing a large leather hat like that with their uniform. We had never seen it in movies, in photos or descriptions of that time in history either.

On April 8, 2010 I was giving a ghost tour and describing the uniform. A guest told me that he was a civil war re-enactor. He was very excited as he told me that the large floppy hat sounded very authentic. He said that the hat is called a slouch hat, and was worn in a variety of ways, including the way that she described. It was always worn by a confederate soldier. It was mostly worn during bad weather, so there would not be a lot of photos of it.

The guest was certain that she saw a real ghost, because her description of the hat was so clear. He said that there was no way that she could have described the slouch hat unless she saw it with her own eyes. If she had imagined or made up the story she would have described a common Kepi hat, which looked much like today's baseball caps.

Civil War Mourners

During the summer of 2009, we had a vender out here installing mattresses in the units. He was staying on property in a unit close to the house. He said that very late on a Wednesday night he couldn't sleep very well, so he got up out of bed to have a cigarette. He noticed that there were two men standing by Eliza's tomb stone. They were dressed as Civil War Union soldiers.

My coworker asked him if he might have seen the fife and drummers who come out here in Revolutionary uniforms to perform on weekends, and he said no. He was sure that they were wearing Civil War attire. Besides, the fife and drummer would not have been out there playing in the middle of the night on a Wednesday, in full uniform. Guests would be sure to complain about that! I heard this story before I found out that the area all around Eliza's grave was a large cemetery with many graves.

Washington Navy Yard, D.C. Edman Spangler, a "conspirator," in slouch hat
and manacled, Library of Congress, C1862

Chapter Six

The Creation of a Vacationer's Paradise

After the Civil War was over the blood was washed clean, the fields were replanted and the house was rebuilt. The slave quarters were gone, and so were the slaves.

The massive fire set by McClellan's men during the Civil War had consumed everything inside of the house, but much of the brick shell remained. The exterior brick, a few of the interior walls and the basement wall and floors are all original to the mansion.

Locals say that all of Dr. Martin's neighbors worked together to repair the war ravaged home for his family, and were done with the repairs in about one year. The Martin family continued to live in the home for over sixty years until his death around the end of the 19th century. (Kibler)

For several years after Dr. Martin died, the house passed through several hands and was in deplorable shape when it was finally purchased by the last man to actually farm the land.

The Last Farmer

The last farmer bought the plantation around 1903. When Mr. Edward M. Slauson purchased the land, the house was uninhabitable. The interior was in such bad condition that you could stand on the bottom floor and see the sky above you. (Kibler) After World War II was over he undertook an extensive restoration of the house. The farmer repaired it with the marks of authenticity.

The Slauson farm with chickens, Source Unknown C1930 – 1942

A friend of mine who grew up in Williamsburg has a beautifully vivid memory of sitting on the front porch steps as a child and sipping homemade lemonade with Mrs. Slauson in the 1960s. To Adrianne's young eyes the home looked just like any normal farm house. It had an old screened in front porch, chickens clucking in the front yard, and weeds growing up all around the fields of corn which surrounded the dairy barns. As a teen she would ride her horse over to the property to hang out with her friends. They would sit and gossip in the warm sunshine for hours, never realizing that the old farm held so many secrets.

She never remembered seeing any ghosts, but she did have a vivid memory of the shape of the roads being very different at that time, and of climbing a huge meandering oak tree outside of the house.

As I sat listening to my friend describe the farm, I was suddenly in awe as I realized that this place was used as a productive plantation consistently from the early 1600s until the Slauson family left in the mid-1970s. This would make it one of the oldest in the nation, after having survived for over 330 years as a productive working farm. Not too many other farms can claim such history.

After the Slauson family left, the mansion and grounds remained vacant for over a decade, until someone had the brilliant idea of integrating the old farm into the development of a new timeshare resort.

Source Unknown C1930 – 39

According to newspaper articles, the resort's original vision for the house was not actually to use it as a showplace, but to utilize it as office space and a community center, surrounded by modern apartments.

The first owners of the resort took great pains to repair the house back into its original splendor. They traveled to England and returned home with a quarter of a million dollars' worth of priceless antiques and quality antique reproduction furniture. Guests always seem shocked when I tell them that it is ok to sit on the sofas, because everything was purchased with the purpose of being used. It seemed that they decorated the house primarily to look pretty, as some of the pieces would not have been used as early as 1735. (Elmore)

Source Unknown, C1930 – 39

I don't know if the previous owners had any paranormal experiences in the house, but employees of this new vacation resort started experiencing paranormal activity as early as 1985.

Haunts in the Units

The timeshare thing turned out to be a very good idea. The original owners purchased 250 acres, and also planned to build a second, smaller resort just a few miles away. Shortly after our resort was built, Williamsburg soon overflowed with countless hotels, motels and timeshares. Our resort grew rapidly along with the commercialism in Williamsburg. Ours was very special though. Besides being the oldest and largest in town, it was also the most beautiful, and had the manor house as its center piece.

Today our timeshare is huge, boasting over 800 units. They are modern, fully functional apartments, stocked with dishes, a washer, dryer and a hot tub. It is booked to capacity with thousands of tourists all summer long and during all major holidays. The resort has been compared to a luxury cruise liner on land, since it has everything here to entertain and divulge in your every need. Many owners stay once a year or more, and their stay is usually for about a week. It is their home away from home.

It is not unusual in the summer months to see the mini-golf course filled with guests, the pools packed with 300 or more sunbathers at a time, and my arts and crafts classes bursting with eager children wanting to make a necklace or finger paint. My job was to entertain and make smiles and I thoroughly enjoyed it. In the bright July days filled with families having fun, it is hard to imagine the secrets that lurked in the depths of the house and the land that surrounds it.

Keep in mind that just because a building is new, clean and beautifully decorated, does not mean that it is free of ghosts. A new home may contain residual energy or spirits from a former time. A new building could also contain an artifact that a spirit has attached itself to, such as an antique piece of furniture. When you think of it this way, it makes absolutely no sense to be afraid of a haunted location, since ghosts are actually all around us at all times, according to this theory.

Look at it this way. Let's say that I own this amazing antique hutch that my Grandma Hazel gave to me. I give my husband very explicit instructions to keep the hutch in the family after I die, so that Halee can enjoy it for years to come. After my death I stay nearby to keep an eye on the husband, kids and my belongings, because I love them all so much, but much to my dismay the scoundrel sells the piece to an antique dealer to get himself a new riding lawnmower.

You buy the hutch from the dealer, but you get much more than a hutch. You will get one ticked off dead tour guide with it! I am sure that I would haunt my husband too, and talk in his ear all night long just for revenge.

Regardless of my personal beliefs about ghosts, I tend to avoid discussing the paranormal activity that occurs inside of the units while talking to our guests in person. I worry that it might upset some folks to think that ghosts could be somewhere other than in the Manor House itself. It is important however for me to remain honest, so when someone asks I will answer them as simply as possible. I always make it very clear that no one has ever been harmed and that there is nothing to be afraid of.

I like to explain that what they are seeing is most likely just a residual echo of something that may have happened here many years ago. I make it clear as well that Williamsburg is very old and many homes and hotels are haunted, not just our resort.

A photo taken of the farm house after it had been abandoned for a decade.
Source Unknown, C 1983

I should mention that if you go on line and do a search for ghosts and include the name of this resort you will not find a whole lot of information about our apparitions. The various resort

74

owners over the years have kept this a secret for a very long time. However, if you search hard enough you can find blogs, photos and stories about us on line.

I was eventually given corporate approval to create my own page on Facebook called "Ghost Journals of a Haunted Manor House", which I used as a daily blog about the tours for a few years. I had to agree not to name the resort of course, but guests were permitted to share their own stories, post photos and videos, including anything they may have seen in their room. Some of the videos were pretty amazing. As far as I know you can still access this blog, even if you are not a member of Facebook.

I know you really want to hear about the ghosts in the units, so twist my arm and I will share a few of the stories about them with you now, since you won't get them out of me during a tour. And just so you know, no matter how hard you twist I will not tell you which ones are haunted. You have to figure that out on your own.

One September afternoon in 2011, I was setting up to teach a soap making class when a guest approached me. A co-worker had sent her to me because the woman was quite upset. I really didn't have time to talk to her since I was expecting a large class, but when my co-worker told me how scared she was I invited her to sit with me and tell me her story. I am glad that I did, as she was visibly shaking and on the verge of tears.

The previous night she woke to find a strange man standing at the foot of her bed. She said that he was transparent. She could not tell what type of clothing he was wearing, but he had longish mussed up hair, was scruffy and seemed sort of angry. As she silently stared at him he said, "My name is James." She watched him disappear in front of her eyes.

She softly asked me if this place was haunted. I knew that she was afraid that I would laugh or say something rude. I told her instead that many people believe that it is, and that she is NOT crazy. I assured her that it would not hurt her, and shared a few other stories with her so that she wouldn't feel so alone in her experience. Obviously she felt better after our talk because she stayed for the rest of the week. She told me that she will come back next year because she wants to see another ghost.

Another story includes a maintenance man going into a unit to do some repair work. As he was working he turned around and saw the figure of a woman staring at him. She disappeared as she walked away.

In some units footsteps of children are heard scurrying up and down the stairs, or across the floor in empty upper rooms. Other reports are vaguer, and simply describe visitors waking to find shadows of people in their rooms, or hearing knocking sounds in the middle of the night.

Last month, a cute little 6 year old and his three siblings calmly informed me that they saw a ghost dog standing by their bed in the middle of the night. Even his baby sister chimed in about the doggy ghost. I looked over at their mother and she just rolled her eyes. I took that as a sign not to press the subject, so I let it drop. Their mother's expression was of exasperation. I guessed that either she was tired of the subject, or maybe she just needed a glass of wine and a hot bath.

Yesterday I was drawing a portrait of this attractive young couple from New York. I was making my usual chit chat while I was doing the sketch, and out of the blue the man asked if the resort was haunted. Without hesitation I said that it was.

He got very excited and started jumping up and down while I was trying to draw him. When he calmed down he told me that on two occasions they were sitting in the living room and the bathroom door just opened on its own.

He was not real pleased that our manor house was closed for renovations, but they promised to come back in a few months to take the tour since he was so excited to have seen something in his bathroom.

I'm not too sure if the sketch looked like him or not, since I didn't get a very good look at him. It's hard to draw a grown man who is screaming and jumping up and down.

Like this man, most of the time witnesses are very excited to have had the experience of seeing a real ghost while vacationing at our resort. I have had more than one guest approach me and complain to me how disappointed they were that they didn't get to see a ghost, as if I had some sort of control over their appearance. I guess they think that I am like some kind of ghost agent or something. I always apologize anyhow as they walk away, shaking their heads. If you have ever worked at a resort or hotel you know that you get really good at apologizing for stuff you didn't do.

The Kitchen during a rare snow storm,
Emily Christoff Flowers, 2011

Ghouls in the Kitchen

The original kitchen to the plantation would have been located close to the house, but in a separate building. There were three reasons why a southern plantation home would have been separated from the kitchen. First, and most importantly, it would have been for fear of fire. Also, the heat of the kitchen would have been unbearable in the hot, muggy southern summers. Finally, there would have been a horrific stench in the kitchen. It would have been so smoky that you could have hung raw meat on the rafters and it would cure. I doubt that it would be overly clean, and let's not even talk about the bugs, Yuk! I wouldn't want that near my house either.

The history of this kitchen building is very interesting. Other than the manor house, it is the only other original building left from the farming days. As early as possibly1903 farmer Slauson and his family built this small house on top of the foundations of the original kitchen. This is where they lived as they were waiting for the completion of the final restorations of the larger house. When they were able to move into the rebuilt home in 1948 they turned this little home into a bed and breakfast.

I am certain that this small dwelling was built on top of the remains of the old kitchen, because in an old newspaper article, written by J. Luther Kibler, Mr. Slauson said that this building had a very large fireplace, in which there hung a heavy iron crane for pots and kettles. He built the new structure around the fireplace and chimney, and gave the crane to Dr. Joseph D. Eggleston, of Hampton-Sydney College. He prized it as an old family heirloom. Dr. Eggleston was a great-great grandson of Richard Eggleston of the early Burgess Egglestons. (Kibler)

When the owners of the new timeshare purchased the land, they decided to salvage this building and turn it into a small posh restaurant, similar to the restaurants that visitors might find in Colonial Williamsburg. Today, diners come from far and wide to enjoy a lavish fireside meal. This restaurant is open to the public, so check it out someday. Maybe you can share your desert with a ghost!

The Kitchen Restaurant has had many interesting paranormal events over the years. I have heard murmurs of waitresses setting up a table only to return a few minutes later to find that all of the glasses were turned upside down. Footsteps of children have also been heard upstairs when no one else was in the building. I had a personal experience in there too, but I'm getting ahead of myself with my stories again.

The building is often used for employee meetings. One friend told me that once she was in the Kitchen for meeting in the early morning hours when the entire front desk staff witnessed a paranormal occurrence.

The building was empty except for Irene and her coworkers. The meeting was just getting started on the first floor, when suddenly they heard the water faucet turn on above them on the second floor. One of them ran up to see who was trying to scare them, but the second floor was empty. The employees felt pretty certain that it was the ghost of a former servant or kitchen slave, attempting to get their attention.

A photo taken of the Kitchen Restaurant
before the resort bought the farm.
Source unknown, C 1983

Lost Graveyards

When they first started construction of the timeshare in 1984, they did not realize that they were building a parking lot over a long lost graveyard.

I want to make it very clear that at the time that this property was purchased to be used as a resort only Eliza's grave remained, and all folk lore concerning the other cemeteries had been long forgotten. Today we maintain her burial site with flowers and a small dignified fence. It sort of makes me mad that a farmer from some other era tore down the other markers. It should come as no surprise to you that there have been so many sightings of ghosts in and around Eliza's grave near the manor house parking lot. I guess they are mad too.

I was very surprised when Matthew found a newspaper article that actually described the two cemeteries on property. One was very old and was surrounded by an old brick wall identical to the wall that surrounds the Bruton Parish church in Williamsburg. By the time that Mr. Slauson found this cemetery all that was left was a few broken markers and the crumbling fence that had been taken over by the roots of a large tree. We do not know where this graveyard was located, but it has been speculated that it was close to where the tennis courts are now. (Virginia Gazette, 1942)

The other was a family cemetery owned by the neighbors, and was referred to simply as the Green Spring family cemetery, or the Ward family cemetery. It was described as being located to the left of the house and near an orchard. According to this article only Eliza H. Ward's marker was left from this once large graveyard when Mr. Slauson bought the property in the early 20th century. We do not know where the other graves are or if they had been moved.

Reenactment from the Other Side

One of the most interesting ghost sightings near the lost graveyard dates back to a spring weekend in 2006. It was a very busy afternoon during check in time. The weather was warm and sunny, and guests were bustling about, getting checked in for the week. Seven different families called the front desk to inquire about the reenactment that they saw by the grave as they were driving onto the property. They did not have time to stop and enjoy it, and so they wanted to know when we were having it again.

Keep in mind that these families did not know each other, however they all saw the same people and described them exactly the same. What they saw was a white female in period colonial clothing, a black older gentleman and a little boy. They were circled around the grave under the tree, just looking at it very sadly as if they were in mourning.

The front desk agents called activities to find out if it was a scheduled event, however there was nothing like that being done on that day. No employees saw the event, only these 7 families. What bugs me about this story is that although I have seen many guests on property wearing colonial clothing for fun, I have never seen a group standing around a grave and pretending to be mourning. Why would anyone go do something like that on their summer vacation? Most folks just go to the amusement park down the street.

19. Powhatan, once owned by Dr. Martin. Located on the . . . . Road, the old road from Jamestown to Williamsburg. Now owned by Mr. E. M. Slauson.

WM Quartly, C1937

Grand staircase on the first floor, with orbs, Shelley Thacker Millirons, 2008

Stairs leading to the third floor with orbs. Shelley Thacker Millirons, 2008

Chapter Seven

Eliza's Story

Who is the woman buried next to the house? We always just assumed that she was the lady of the house at one time and that she died and was buried next to her home.

I was talking about this one day with a woman who came by to take my watercolor class. It turns out that my student had a love for family history. I guess she wasn't into the amusement parks and waffle houses, because she spent the rest of her vacation in the Williamsburg library digging up information about Eliza. She said it was the highlight of her visit. I wish I still had her name and number to recognize her properly. If you are out there reading this, thank you, thank you, and thank you!

Thanks to her research we now know that Eliza H. Ward, the woman buried next to the house, was actually the wife of a wealthy merchant from New York. They had traveled to this area to vacation with his family, who owned Green Spring plantation. Apparently she become sick or had some kind of accident and died while on their visit and they choose not to return her body to New York, but to bury her in the family plot at the neighbor's house. The tomb stone claims that she passed on in 1849, at the age of 38. Research states that she was buried in a large family plot at our farm, called the Ward Cemetery. We do not believe that she ever set foot inside of the manor house, and so she may not be the ghost whom we call Eliza. (Ancestry.com)

Ghosts don't usually stick around the place that they were buried, but tend to haunt the places that they lived, the people they loved or the places in which they died.

I will be quite honest with you; I don't know who our ghost Eliza was in life. We mistakenly named her after the lonely tomb stone sitting next to the house. I asked a spirit box once what she was named and it said Elizabeth. A psychic also told me that her name was similar to Eliza.

Our ghost could actually have been someone named Elizabeth since there were several women by this name that used to live in the house. We have record of Elizabeth Eggleston, who married Richard Taliaferro. They had a daughter named Elizabeth Wythe, and their son gave them a granddaughter named Elizabeth Taliaferro. Also, since the farm had many servants, nameless tenant farmers and slaves over the years, it could easily be one of them since Elizabeth was a very common name. We still call my favorite spirit Eliza however, since she doesn't seem to mind this name at all.

My ghost Eliza has a special place in my heart. She seems to be the most active entity in the Manor House and has been sighted by countless witnesses throughout the years, long before I met her in 2006. Eliza is described by most witnesses as being petite and light on her feet. She is very sweet and is in charge of the house and all of its occupants.

Several psychics are convinced that she follows me on the ghost tours and that she stands protectively by my side as I address the crowds. They also told me that she often follows me home, but will not follow me down into the basement. She loves me dearly and I am familiar to her as a member of her family

One lady said that Eliza thinks that it is very funny that when I am talking about her during my tours I always gesture up as if she is in heaven, when in reality she is right by my side. I have quite a few photos showing a mist or orb next to me.

Once, another lady was trying to convince me that Eliza was standing right behind me, but I just laughed and shook my head. My back was to a hutch, and the door swung open right at this moment and tapped me gently on the back of my head, causing me to yelp and jump about a foot into the air. I didn't deny Eliza after that.

I have never heard her voice with my own ears, or seen a clear apparition of her, but I do feel a calming female presence in the house. If I am having a bad day, all I need to do is to find a quiet corner in an abandoned room and close my eyes for a few minutes and I can almost feel her soothing arms around my shoulders. Perhaps I am feeling Eliza, or maybe it is just the gentle energy and love of the old farm house calming my nerves.

The Quiet Ghost

Many guests over the years have told stories of seeing a woman wearing a green or blue colonial dress and mop cap inside of the house. We think this could be a description of Eliza.

One lady in fact was so certain that she had seen this ghost that she called the front desk to share her story.

She said that she was walking through the house with her daughter, and this middle aged lady dressed in a colonial style dress walked right by her and totally ignored her when she said hello. The rude woman had light colored hair, glasses and a scarf on her head. The guest assumed that she was a costumed interpreter who had no manners. Her daughter did not see this vision, even though she was standing right next to her mother. Mother did not mention it to her daughter at this time.

The daughter went upstairs alone to look around and saw the same woman, exactly how her mother later described her, sitting on the stairs leading up to the third floor. The lady was staring at her through the spindles of the stairway. The daughter greeted her, but the woman did not respond. She simply continued to stare at her in a very odd way. The daughter also assumed that she was a costumed interpreter waiting on someone to return. What is interesting is that she had a clear view of the woman's shoes. The shoes were handmade leather, identical to the shoes worn during colonial times. She thought that it was very strange for an interpreter to have authentic homemade shoes. Most independent interpreters wear modern shoes since handmade colonial style shoes are very expensive.

It wasn't until much later that the mother and daughter shared their experiences with each other. After comparing notes they got the courage to call the front desk to ask if the house was haunted.

The front desk manager called around to see if there was any costumed interpreters working or visiting that day. She was assured that there were no employees in costume at that time. There were also no accounts of a costumed guest. The mother and daughter concluded that they might have been a witness to a sighting of our dear Eliza.

Some people have speculated that it could have been my boss Iris. She did some costumed interpretations several years ago, and it does sort of describe her. When I think about it though I know that there is no way that it could have been Iris.

She is a very friendly type. She wouldn't have passed up an opportunity to get to know a guest; in fact she would have talked the lady's ear off and made a new friend.

Several years after this incident the same mother and daughter attended one of my tours. They retold the story to me exactly how the front desk manager had recited it.

Eliza Saves Iris

Iris claims that she doesn't believe most ghost stories, but she said that this one particular experience was pretty convincing.

In the mid to late 80s Iris was working as a costumed docent, and did many programs with the guests. She was taking a scheduled break between events on the third floor when she dozed off. She would have gotten into a lot of trouble if she had missed her program because she fell asleep on her lunch break, but she woke to the feeling of a faint burning or warm sensation on the top of her hand, and then it got very cold. It felt like someone was gently stroking her hand as if to wake her up. When Iris opened her eyes she was completely alone on the third floor. It was time for her next event to begin and she arrived to it barely on time.

Iris told me another interesting story describing Eliza that had happened around the same time. A man working for the power or phone company was in the manor house doing some repairs. When he looked up he saw a full body apparition of a woman descending the stairs towards him. She was all white and shimmering and definitely not human. He was so shocked that he ran out of the front door, never to return.

Bad Ghost Service

In the late 1990s a couple was checking in for their stay at the resort. It was around 2:00 am, and they were exhausted from traveling. They saw the lights on in the house and so they approached the front door, assuming that it was the resort registration.

They tried to open the door but it was locked. Thinking that this was odd they took a peak into the first window on the left and saw a woman dressed in a beautiful colonial style gown, pacing the room back and forth. They assumed that this was a costumed employee, so they knocked on the door. The lady ignored them, and so they tried shouting and eventually tapping on the window to get her attention, but she would not even glance up at them.

Now they were really mad. There is nothing worse than poor guest service at a gold star resort! They somehow managed to find the correct desk where they complained about the rude woman. I am sure that the staff apologized profusely for her bad treatment. They eventually got to their room and security was notified. Of course when security got to the house they found it totally empty. Apparently the couple were the victims of poor ghost service.

A Good First Impression

In July of 2009 I was teaching another guest service class to the security team on the third floor apartment of the house. I am still not sure why I was nominated to teach a class on etiquette, since as you may have figured out by now, I tend to have the gift of gab. I made the best of it anyhow, and tried to make the class as interesting as I could.

It is difficult to make the discussion topic of proper grooming and personal hygiene interesting I must admit, so I tried to make the room a little more welcoming by turning off the harsh overhead lights and using soft lamps around the studio.

At the end of the hour long class I gave my parting remark which was, "Don't forget that you only have one chance to make a good first impression." At this very moment the overhead florescent lights flickered on.

For a few heartbeats we all just sat there with our mouths open and starred dumbly at the light and each other. I looked behind me and saw that the only switch to that light was directly behind me with no one standing nearby, and in perfect view of the entire room. When I realized what happened I laughed and thanked Eliza for agreeing with me and for giving us all a good first impression. I thought it was a hoot, but you should have seen how fast those security guards ran out of the house.

Southern Hospitality is a Must

We hire various actors, magicians, clowns and outside vendors to perform at the resort. I figured that if anyone had seen anything interesting in the house it might be the gentleman who does historical reenactments in the home. When I caught up with the actor he was very excited to tell me all about his many odd occurrences with Eliza. He used to have a general discussion about the ghosts of Williamsburg, while portraying John Rollison, a free black man who lived in the mid-18th century.

He explained that his first encounter was on a quiet autumn night. He had a small group lingering after his performance. They were all in the main lobby near the stairs when he heard footsteps on the second floor. He assumed of course that it was just someone from his group taking a last look around or using the restroom. When everyone left he was still waiting for her to come down so that he could leave for the night. He eventually lost patience and went back upstairs to check on her. When he got to the second floor he was quite puzzled to find it empty and dark.

He noticed that the bathroom door was closed with the light on, so he knocked and then carefully opened it. It was empty as well. Shrugging his shoulders he figured that she had just slipped past him and out the door, so he walked back down to the first floor and finished gathering his belongings.

Just as he was getting ready to leave for the night he heard the same shuffling footsteps again. It could not have been mistaken for natural noises; it was definitely solid footsteps of a human. He felt like Eliza was playing with him and trying to scare him, so he quickly left the house.

A few weeks later he was alone in the house once again, standing at the base of the grand stairs on the first floor. His performance went well, and all of his guests had already left for the night. As he began cleaning up he felt a tremendous chill and his hair stood up on his arms. It stunned him. It came out of the blue. It felt like he had upset the ghost, but he couldn't figure out how.

He suddenly realized that he had never thanked Eliza for allowing him to take advantage of her home and her southern hospitality. From this point on, for the next several years, he always ended his shows by saying, "Goodnight Eliza, may the good Lord bless you, keep you and comfort you.

The guests heard an odd noise in the corner of the room which sounded like a chair being moved, Kelly Robbins turned quickly and snapped this photo. She captured a small mist on the pillow. 2010

Chapter Eight

Shadow Figures Creeping Through the House

What are shadow figures and where do they come from? Several theories have been bounced around by smart people, but we still don't know for sure. Skeptics and mainstream science usually write this off as being a figment of an over active imagination. They claim that is simply our minds playing tricks on us, or our eyes seeing real shadows caused by passing cars or a cloud. I am sure that these explanations can account for some of our sightings, but not of all of them, especially when some of these shadows have been captured on film and seen by multiple witnesses in the house.

Shadow figures are different than your usual ghost apparitions, who usually have the appearance of being misty white, and are often seen wearing clothing and having clear facial features. Shadow figures are usually much darker and have no distinct features. They sometimes appear out of the corner of your eye, but on a few occasions people claim to have seen them directly in front of them. In the manor house, most guests seem to see them flickering up and down the stair way, at unusually quick speeds. I personally have seen them up the stairs as well as appearing directly in front of me on the second floor.

A Shadow Turns Off the Light

My assistant, Vicky, was hosting an evening tour of about 35 guests on Monday, September 20, 2010. Vicky did not believe in ghosts, but she did repeat to me events that would happen on her tours, if the guest seemed genuine and honest about their experience. In some cases she even experienced phenomenon as well, but it was never enough to convince her of their authenticity. Vicky is a very smart girl, but she refused to accept the ghosts even when they appeared during her tours. A ghost could have jumped up in her face and slapped her silly, but she would have found some other explanation for what she saw. She was a good guide though, and I trusted her completely and liked her a lot. I respected her for sticking to her beliefs.

I saw this neat trick on TV and wanted to try it on the tour. I will explain more about it later, but for now just know that our ghosts like to turn our flashlight off and on during the tours.

Vicky whole heartedly felt that the flashlight phenomenon was not paranormal, but was the effect of some physical mechanical problem with the batteries. She always shared this opinion with the guests, but it usually did not stop them from becoming excited if the light would flash on and off on command. It doesn't do it during every tour, and it had not happened with Vicky in several weeks.

While the group was in the game room, attempting to coax the flashlight on, there were two ladies sitting on the love seat being chatty. One of them blurted out that behind the gentleman wearing a baseball cap, there was a shadow figure of a 6 foot tall man, and another shadow about 5 feet tall. They said that these figures were standing near the traveling chest opposite of the entrance to the room and that their feet were not touching the ground.

Vicky looked but did not see anything except for the shadows created by the other people in the room. Apparently the only people who could see these ghosts were the two women. She did not believe that it was a sighting of a shadow ghost, but to appease the women she asked the shadow to please turn off the flashlight. The room turned silent as the light flashed off. Even Vicky was impressed.

Is It A Ghost or a Guest?

I want you to know that Charles is not a coward. He may look like a sweetheart, but I knew that he could kick the butt of Chuck Norris if he wanted to. He even showed me a photo once of when he was in a movie as a martial artist stunt double, dressed as some sort of turtle. Since I knew that he was a highly trained martial artist and a former cop, you can imagine my surprise when I heard that he would not enter the house, due to a horrific encounter he had once with a shadow ghost.

The front yard looking away from the house towards the woods and former slave quarters. Shelley Thacker Millirons, 2010

One night, sometime after midnight, he was driving around property doing a routine security sweep. He noticed what looked like a man stalking around the outside of the manor house. When he took a closer look he realized that it was a not a man, but the shadow of a large translucent entity. He couldn't believe his eyes.

He gathered his courage and approached the shadow, but it began to run. He chased it around the house as he called

95

for backup, but it moved too fast for him to keep up with it. As Charles rounded the corner of the house it was gone.

From that moment on he decided that he is going to avoid going into the manor house at all costs. This would pose a problem at night however since he is required to search the house for guests before locking it up.

He came up with a compromise. He decided that instead of actually entering the home, he would just poke his head in the front door and shout loudly to see if anyone was there. If he didn't get a response then he would lock it up. It seemed like a great idea at the time.

This plan worked well for a while but one night he had a very bad shock. He opened the door, peered into the dark front hall and shouted, "Is anyone in here?" Just as he was about to lock the house and run he nearly jumped out of his skin when a very loud voice shouted back, "I'm here!" from just behind the door.

Much to Charles' embarrassment it turned out to be a guest, not a ghost!

A Shadow Hiding Behind Mom

I always encourage guests to speak up if they see anything odd while they are on the tours. In April of 2010 a guest told me that a few days prior to the tour she, her husband and her 2 adult sons went up to the second floor to look around. While she was standing alone in the dining room she felt someone walk very closely behind her. She thought it might be her husband, but when she turned around and saw that he and the sons were standing in a room across the hall. She was alone in the room.

One son looked over at her just at this moment and saw a dark shadow of a tall man walking behind her and across the foyer into the library. This story excited me since they told this to me before they learned that I saw the exact same ghost in the very same location several years prior.

About a month after this incident another mother and her two young daughters approached me before a tour to tell me that they had seen a shadow figure in the house. They were out taking a walk when it started to rain. The family ducked into the house to escape from the storm when they glanced up towards the dim stairway and all three of them saw a very fast moving human looking shadow racing up the stairs. Mom asked the girls if they just saw something and they started to whimper, describing the shadow exactly how their mother had seen it. They decided to leave and come back with a group, hoping that they would have the courage to walk all the way through the house if they were not alone.

A photo of the basement taken during a ghost tour.
Some people see faces and shadows in the corner.

A photo taken during a prank that shows orbs. Notice Jon's reflection in the mirror on the chair .He was sitting behind the table with the gingerbread house.
Photo by Virginia Christoff, 2007

Chapter Nine

Pranks on the Living

I have discovered over time that Eliza and her unearthly friends have a delightful sense of humor and love it when we play pranks on each other. Sometimes they even like to play along or amuse themselves by creating their own harmless mischief. I thought that you would enjoy knowing that all of us employees have a good sense of humor about our ghosts and don't take them too seriously all of the time. As you will see, the ghosts obviously feel the same way about us.

My Brother is a Chicken

I come from a family with an abundance of kids, and we are still always trying to get each other's goat. My little brother Tony is the youngest of 7, and so I guess he thinks he can still get away with teasing his big sister, even into our adult years. He had been teasing me quite a bit lately about seeing ghosts at my new job, and I was getting a bit perturbed with him for suggesting that I might be going a little crazy in my old age.

When he and our mother Ginny came down for a visit from Ohio in February of 2007, Tony asked if I could give him a tour of the "haunted house". This was my chance to get back at him and I started making my plans to play a most wonderful prank on him in revenge. Poor Mom is often the brunt of her kid's pranks too, so I decided to let her in on the joke in advance. She was tickled pink.

I arranged for the curator Belinda to give him a theatrical "ghost tour" of the house. This was long before I had developed the actual tour, so I was very excited to play along and see what happened. Of course Tony had no idea that Belinda was making it all up, he thought her stories were legitimate. Mom and I knew better.

Since it was an overcast winter afternoon the house was quiet, dark and damp. For the first part of her tour she made up some very gory stories as she walked us through the rooms. We noticed that as Tony became more and more excited about these fabricated tales that the lights in the house actually started to flicker. We passed through some cold spots and our hair stood up on end on a few occasions too. By the time we got to the last room, Tony was beside himself with anxiety and his face was turning red. I was hiding a smile and silently thanking Eliza for playing along. Oh yeah, this was going to be real good!

My trap was already set. My co-worker Jon had a great idea to give Tony a real jolt. He was hiding behind a large table decked out with a ginger bread house in the library room. He was dressed in 18th century clothing that resembled the clothing worn by the man in the portrait hanging above the mantel right above him. The table hid Jon so well that you could not see him from the door, but you could however see him in a mirror which he carefully placed in the corner, next to a pillow, to capture his reflection. Since the lights were off, the room was very dim and quiet. At first glance it appeared that the room was empty. The curator explained to Tony that you could not walk into the room or you would fall through the floor. The rope was across the door for his safety. Of course was a total lie.

As Tony stared into the gloom of the Library, Belinda told a bogus story about the man in the portrait. We actually do not know who the model is, but the curator told Tony that the man in the painting was a murderer who savagely killed his family with an axe in the house many years ago. She added that if you ever see his reflection in a mirror it meant that you are about to die. She made this up on the spot, and I thought it was pretty brilliant.

It was at this point that my baby brother saw Jon's pale face reflected in the mirror. He screamed, pointed and asked if I could see it. I said, "Gee Tony, I don't see anything."

Mom just batted her eyelashes and assured him that he was just seeing things.

Tony started to tremor and cough, and shouted for mom to start taking photos. Mom obliged him by taking about 10 photos consecutively, while attempting to hold back a giggle.

We were all trying very hard not to laugh when a family came upstairs and peered into the room. When they first saw Jon they whispered to me that they saw a man in the mirror holding his finger over his lips, and going shhhhhhh. Fortunately my brother didn't hear this comment. They realized pretty quickly that this was a joke so they told Tony that they didn't see a face in the mirror either, and that Tony must be going crazy. This unexpected twist from these wonderful strangers really took the prank up another notch. Ah, sweet revenge.

Jon started to shake silently with laughter, his eyes filling with tears of suppressed glee. My brother clutched his chest and screamed, "Oh my God, it's having a seizure and its crying!"

Tony jumped over the rope, all thoughts of falling through the floor forgotten. Young Jon, fearing for his life, quickly stood up and said, "Hey dude, don't hurt me, it was just a joke. It was all your sisters' idea, not mine!" Jon pointed at me and Tony grew silent and slowly turned towards me to see if it was true. I fell on the floor laughing. Tony has yet to forgive me.

What was really freaky however was that when we looked at Mom's photos the next day, one photo showed Jon's reflection with glowing orbs surrounding him, the other 9 photos had no orbs. It was obvious that the ghosts were in on the joke too.

Keep the Lights Off

I was leaving work one December night in 2006 when I had a very upsetting encounter with Eliza. Since it was already dark outside, I had left the light on over the third floor stairs so that I could see to make my way down the narrow staircase. We always kept the lights off in the house at this time, and so the rest of the house was full of shifting shadows and reflections of the cars coming down the main road.

As soon as I locked the art studio door and turned around, the light over my head turned off. This left me standing alone in the darkness. I nearly passed out in shock.

At first I thought it was a guest turning off the lights from the switch at the bottom of the stairs, but I could tell from the dim light coming in from the street that there was no one there. The only other switch was in the empty room that I had just locked. I checked to see if the light bulb had burned out, but when I turned the switch back on it worked perfectly. I carefully made my way out of the dark house, feeling like something was following close behind me.

I found out later from Belinda that Eliza likes to tease the security team by turning on the lights in the middle of the night. I guess that the midnight shift would see that the lights were on and key into the house and turn them all off. They would lock the house up as they were leaving, only to look over their shoulder and see that the house was all lit up again.

She said that she had asked Eliza to stop harassing them and to keep the lights off after we leave. I think that Eliza was either teasing me or she was taking the curator's request a bit too seriously.

Now we leave the lights on all during the night. Besides being very pretty, it also keeps the ghosts from teasing security.

Busted

One afternoon in May of 2009 I went up to the third floor to grab some supply for Iris. By this time our arts and crafts studio had been moved to another building, so I didn't get to visit the house too often. I took a seat in a very comfortable chair, put my feet up and pulled my cell phone out to make a call to my sister I don't usually mess around on the clock, but I figured that I could call her quickly and no one would know since I was alone in the house.

As I was talking to her I heard footsteps coming up the stairs and approaching the closed door. My first thought was that

I was busted by Iris gabbing on my phone, so I asked Melissa to hold on while I hid my cell and stood by the door. A firm hand knocked on the door and I immediately opened it.

The stairway was empty. There was no sound coming from anywhere inside of the house, and certainly the person who had knocked did not have time to run down the stairs and hide.

I realized that Eliza was reminding me to get back to work, or was playing one of her harmless pranks on me. I returned to my sister who heard the entire event. She asked who it was and I calmly told her that it was just a ghost playing with me. She screamed, "Run for it! Get the heck out of there!" I laughed and assured her that Eliza was just having fun. My sister assured me that I was crazy.

The Headless Zombie

I know that I joke about my new boss Iris a lot, but please know that I think very highly of her. Iris likes to say that she is not afraid of ghosts. We all deal with the paranormal aspects of the house in our own way, but I suspected that Iris was more afraid than she let on, and I was about to prove it. This is not a ghost story exactly, but it is very funny.

I heard a rumor that Iris had set up a fake ghost as a prank in the third floor studio. The Halloween costume of a headless zombie was very well made and consisted of a long robe, a bloody stump of a neck which is worn on top of the wearers head like a hat, and a rubber hand grasping a cut off head like a football. The head is actually a puppet, and you can move its lips with your hand. The person wearing it can see very clearly out of a little hidden window, but the victim cannot see the body or face of the person wearing the costume. My son Eddie loves to wear this costume as he passes out treats to the kids at our annual Halloween party.

Iris, being the prankster that she is, had posed this full body headless zombie costume on a sewing manikin in the corner of one of the third floor studio rooms. Every time someone would see it during a staff meeting they would scream and run out of the room as Iris and the rest of the employees stood back and laughed at them. The room is used quite frequently; so many people were the victims of her foul joke. I was warned that she was going to try to scare me eventually, so I began to prepare for my counter attack.

Iris asked to meet me and my coworker Eric up in the studio one afternoon. She told me it was to help her dig up some supplies out of a closet, but I knew that she was actually setting me up for the prank. Eric and I arrived a few minutes early; I put on the costume, hid the manikin and stood quietly in the dark corner in its place. I looked just like the manikin with the costume on it as long as I didn't move or sneeze.

I was standing very still, barely daring to breathe, when I heard my boss trudge up the stairs and enter the room. Eric told her that I was running late, and Iris said, "Oh good, let me show you this zombie I put up here to scare people. I want to try to scare Em!" I heard her follow this with an evil laugh.

Iris walked into the room and said, "Em will turn the corner like this see, and the lights will be off. When she sees this thing in the corner she will think it is one of her ghosts, and then she will scream!" I could see Iris's grin through the window of my costume, her eyes sparkling with anticipation.

"It will be great!" she giggled as she walked towards me. "Finally, we can see her scared to death!"

Iris was so close to me now that she started to fuss with the fabric of my robe and re-arrange it on what she thought was the manikin. Just at that moment I took a step forward and reached for her with the bloody head. I growled like a zombie, and started stomping around and shaking the decapitated head at her. I could see her stunned face through the little window, but she could not see me.

She screamed, grabbed her heart and stumbled backwards and yelled, "No, oh my God, no!"

I realized that I may have gone too far. I said, "Iris, are you OK?" I reached out to steady her as she fought to gain control of her legs, but this only frightened her more. She thought

104

the zombie was trying to catch and eat her I guess. She gasped for air and started hyperventilating. Oh man, if Iris survived this I was so fired!

I tore off the costume as quickly as I could, fearing that I had given my boss a heart attack, and then she immediately recognized me.

There was a long moment of silence.

Her confused mind tried to grasp what had just happened, and then, much to my relief, she burst into gales of laughter. We laughed for a solid ten minutes.

She has yet to fire me, and I think she has since forgiven me. Having a playful sense of humor is a wonderful way to deal with the stress of working in a haunted house.

The Spirits Play Along

I find it incredibly humorous that security likes to initiate new guards by telling them scary stories while walking through the old house after dark. One late night in the middle of winter, Caleb followed his supervisor Diana to the second floor. Diana was having a hard time scaring him since he claimed to be a firm non believer in anything supernatural. He thought the stories were very funny however, so he began making fun of the ghosts and pretending to talk to them. His supervisor warned him to stop, but the new employee was having way too much fun.

As they walked next to the open bathroom door the light suddenly turned on, although the room was empty. Caleb's good mood was dampened some, but he still did not believe.

Several weeks later he was walking alone through the house at night, preparing to lock it up. He noticed that the same bathroom door was shut and locked with the light still on. He knocked first to make sure that it was not occupied, but then he became quite annoyed when he realized that he had left the key all the way back at the security shack. First he tried jiggling the handle, then he tried to force the door open, but nothing would budge the door.

Caleb had an idea. If the ghosts were real, maybe they could help him out and open the door for him to save him the trouble of taking the long walk all the way back for the key. He looked around first to make sure that no one could see him, after all he didn't want people to think he was nuts like that ghost lady tour guide. He turned towards the door and softly asked Miss Eliza if she could please open the door for him. He paused a minute then laughed at himself for being a fool. Of course the door didn't open, what was he thinking?

He started to saunter back down the stairs when he realized that he never pulled on the door to see if it worked, so he headed back over to the bathroom. Much to his astonishment the door opened for him. Caleb is a believer now.

Stalking Security

Caleb's supervisor was locking up the house one early spring night and doing her sweep to make sure that everyone had left the house for the day. It was only a few weeks prior to that when she had taken the new guard through the house in an attempt to scare him, so I think perhaps the ghosts wanted to give her a taste of her own medicine.

After making her way through the silent house she locked the third floor door and turned around to descend the stairs. Diana immediately heard footsteps right behind her coming from the top of the stairs. This was impossible; the few feet behind her were empty and the door was locked. She continued down the stairs and pretended not to notice the footsteps behind her, hoping that she was simply hearing the stairs shift with her own weight.

When she got to the second floor landing, the footsteps were only a few feet behind and getting closer. Her heart began to race, but she knew that she had to remain calm. She had read that when a human shows fear that ghosts can get stronger from their energy, and she didn't want this to happen. She simply started the long descent to the bottom floor. She was certain that she would be pushed from behind by unseen hands, and so she stepped slowly, while firmly grasping the hand rail.

This time the footsteps were closer than before. It was almost like they were walking in step with her, taunting or teasing her. When she walked they walked. When she stopped they stopped. It was the strangest thing she had ever experienced.

At this point she mustered up all of her courage, turned around and said, "OK, well, you have a good night." Then she bolted for the door, the invisible feet following close behind.

She tore open the front door and slammed it behind her, but her curiosity got the best of her. Holding her breath she cracked the door open for a final peek back into the house. The footsteps were still coming across the floor towards her, as if they were going to join her outside. She slammed the door as fast as she could, locked it up with shaking hands and ran.

The ghosts were apparently not done giving Diana a hard time. A few months after she was chased through the house she had to unlock it for the day. It was around 8:00 am, and she knew that no one was inside, however as she was just about to insert the key, the door knob began to jiggle. It was as if someone was about to open the door from inside and walk out towards her. She took a step back. She was a little confused at first, and then she realized that Caleb must be trying to get back at her for trying to scare him on his first day of work. He was obviously inside of the door expecting her to scream when she opened it.

She decided to unlock it quickly and jump inside to startle whoever was playing this joke on her. Totally expecting to see an ornery co-worker hiding inside, she quickly opened the door, bounded inside and prepared to say "Boo". The words died on her lips. The house was empty.

Fingers on the Harpsichord

As I mentioned before, the first builders of the resort filled the Manor House with priceless antiques when they were renovating it in 1984. One of our most cherished pieces is a miniature harpsichord called a Bentside Spinet.

Most wealthy homes had harpsichords during the 18th century, and so it stands to reason that Mrs. Taliaferro may have had one as well. A harpsichord is the grandmother of today's piano, and is played in very much the same way. Women were limited when it came to playing musical instruments, but this beautiful keyboard was considered a woman's instrument.

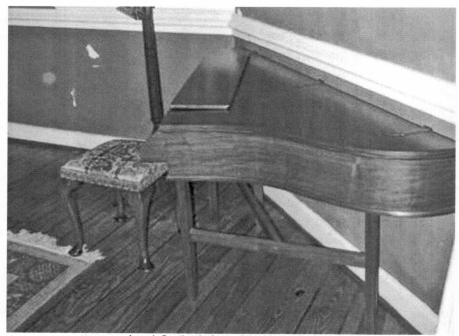
An orb floating in front of the Harpsichord,
Emily Christoff Flowers, 2010

Women had very odd rules of modesty during the 18th century. As a colonial woman, Elizabeth Taliaferro was only permitted to participate in modest activities that would not expose certain parts of her body while in the public eye. An exposed female elbow or ankle could send a man into a fit of passion during her time. Cleavage was OK, just don't show that elbow, go figure. Usually when I say this on a tour I notice at least one woman roll up her sleeves and glance slyly at her man.

A woman was permitted to play the harpsichord because she did not raise her arms while doing so, thus she did not expose those naughty elbows. Oftentimes this instrument would also include a fabric skirt, to hide the woman's exposed ankles.

Speaking of colonial music, my little brother Stephen came to visit me in Williamsburg fifteen years ago. He liked it so much that he stayed and got a job here as a balladeer for Colonial Williamsburg. I think Mom and Dad might still be a little mad at me about that. You ought to know that although I call him "little", he is actually six foot 5 or so. He is a gentle giant though, and loves to come to hang out with us, especially around dinner time.

When performing he plays his guitar or mandolin in the taverns during meals and special events, and he sings with the most beautiful golden voice. Part of his job is to study colonial performance, and I love to pick his musical brain.

He patiently explained to me that music was a huge part of colonial life. For example, slaves brought a wealth of musical knowledge with them from Africa. They took a hallow gourd, attached a stick to it and fixed cat gut strings to the stick. They covered the gourd with animal hide and plucked the strings.

I thought Stevie was pulling my leg, so I looked it up and sure enough Thomas Jefferson was one of the first people to make note of this new musical instrument in 1871. He called it the banjar. Today you and I call it the banjo. (Reese)

Stevie also called me one evening and proudly announced that he has a brand new sackbut. I told him that I was very happy for him, figuring that perhaps he was referring to a new girlfriend. He quickly corrected me by saying that a Sackbut was a colonial trombone, played only by the very wealthiest of men. Plantation owners would gather in the gentleman's parlor, sip their hard cider, smoke their tobacco pipes and play in what they called Sackbut guilds. I wonder if Col. Taliaferro was a professional sackbutter.

We think that Elizabeth and Richard could still be teasing us by playing their music after death. Many guests over the years have claimed to hear a single note being played softly on the harpsichord as they are in an adjoining room. One fall evening a guest was taking a late night stroll, when he walked past the music room under the window closest to the harpsichord. He heard it being played very clearly and so he called security to unlock the house and check it out.

First security walked under the window to see if they could hear anything. They also heard someone playing the keyboard. They rushed into the house to catch the invader, but the house was empty. They did a full search, but it was silent and unoccupied.

Chapter Ten

The Ghost Tours

Finally, after months of research, interviews and writing, I was ready to start the new ghost tours. Now, remember that Iris had to poke and prod me into doing them and so I was sort of lukewarm about them at first. It's true that I had seen crazy things and had heard all sorts of bizarre stories about the house before starting my journey, but there was still a very skeptical part of me that was not one hundred percent convinced. There was also that memory of being ridiculed as a child that made me fear a little bit about how people would accept the topic. I seriously doubted that the few people who I thought would attend would even enjoy it.

Most of the stories I have told you about so far occurred during the several years that I worked here before I started doing my new event. I had not really seen anything spectacular happen in the house for a while before I started bringing guests through it, so I was blown over when I started witnessing paranormal activity in the house on almost every tour. In fact, my first tour left me breathless.

The Ghost Who Followed Me Home

On March 11, 2010, I was walking alone through the house, memorizing my notes, when a family approached and asked if they could tag along and listen. I thought it was a great idea since I was quite nervous and hoped that it would help me to prepare for the group that I was expecting the next day.

As I started telling my stories the family became anxious. We were upstairs in the Library room when the son shouted that the doors to the hutch behind the dining room table had just popped open. Shortly after that, his dad jumped and said that something very cold just blew on the back of his neck, and it wasn't his wife.

About five minutes later mom yelped. She giggled to cover her nerves, and then explained that her purse had just been tugged on from behind; even though no one was standing near her.

The family was excited, but very quick to leave the house and its invisible occupants. Obviously the ghosts liked my first tour because one of them followed me home that evening.

Later that night, as I was snoring away in bed, my fat tabby Sophia started to cry. I woke my sleeping husband and asked him to lock the cat up into the garage. I am very grumpy when I am awoken from a sound sleep. What is really funny about all of this is that my man claimed to be a non–believer and a total ghost skeptic. He is a very traditional real life cowboy from Texas, a Navy Vet and afraid of nothing. What he saw in our home that night however changed his mind forever about the paranormal, and gave him a bit of a start.

As David entered the dark hallway searching for our cat, he saw a bright orange glowing orb floating above poor Sophia. It slowly meandered down the hall towards the kitchen, turned the corner and vanished!

This would not be the last time that a ghost would follow me home after a tour. Strangely enough the thought of one of the ghosts following me home didn't bug any of us at all. Well, at least it didn't bug us much until later.

After this first experience we often noticed our dog Bailey staring and whining at an empty seat or a corner of the house. Both pet's eyes would follow in unison an invisible person walking through the room. It is not unusual to hear footsteps, have electronic equipment in our home go crazy and have lights flicker. I have even caught this bizarre phenomenon on video during one of Lucy's visits to our home. Our lights were flickering and we could hear knocking sounds come from the back door. We were a bit scared!

Sometimes when I am at home doing studio work I will see one necklace out of my huge display of crafting beads sway in a nonexistent breeze, things will mysteriously fall off of counters, or

I feel someone standing behind me when I am busy painting. David is a believer now and no longer teases me when I bring home stories from work. The kids thought it was cool too. When they grew older they even became ghost tour guides with me.

The tours would be sold out almost every day, week after week. Some nights were simply crazy. Guests would become infuriated if they were put on a waiting list. I soon found out that some people would do absolutely anything to sneak on one of my sold out tours.

The little event that I intended to do once a week for a small handful of history buffs soon turned out to be the most attended reoccurring event at the resort. Suddenly I found myself doing less art classes and portrait drawing, and focusing almost totally on the tours. We even tried getting people to help me, but many of my coworkers were not willing to step foot in the house let alone wander around the mansion with the lights off after dark.

I loved the recognition that I received for all of my hard work. I even got awarded as resort employee of the month for all of my efforts. I keep this certificate above my desk. I must admit however that nothing could have pleased me more than to realize that the ghosts seemed to love my work also.

The most astounding thing was that the equipment that I brought along to entertain the younger kids on the tours would actually succeed in detecting and communicating with ghosts. You see, I didn't believe in all of that. I always assumed that the meters, ghost boxes and all the hoopla on TV was just a hoax. I soon discovered that I could communicate with Eliza and that Eliza was my friend. The equipment was no hoax.

As the tours progressed I realized that it seemed as if the ghosts were being energized by our visits. This phenomenon made sense once I researched that spirits can become more energetic if they are around people who are displaying strong emotions. (Balzano)

The Flashlight

One of the most interesting tricks for communicating with ghosts on those reality shows is actually very simple. The investigators use a flashlight that turns on with a twist instead of a button. They twist the flashlight so that it is right between on and off, then ask it questions. If the flashlight flickers or changes it is allegedly a response from the spirit world, and the reality star will respond with, "Dude, it's a ghost!"

Of course I always thought it was a bunch of doo doo, but found it highly entertaining. I figured I would get a little flashlight and try it for myself during the tours anyhow, just for kicks. I told my visitors not to expect the light to work.

For the first several months of the tours I set the flashlight down in the second floor foyer as I explained the theory. It came as no surprise to me that it never worked. The guests seemed to appreciate it though, and it was a lot of fun. Eventually I needed to change the order of a few of my stories and so one afternoon I moved the experiment into the game room.

It was a packed tour that day, and there was barely enough room to fit everyone around the little table that held the flashlight. After turning it on I took a few steps back and asked Eliza to please turn it off if she was with us in the room. As usual the flashlight remained unchanged, and so I moved the group into the next room, leaving the flashlight sitting on the table.

A few minutes later I heard a blood curdling screech from the game room. I ran back into the room to see a man and his wife talking excitedly. He kept pointing to the flashlight and stuttering that it was haunted! I glanced at the light and it was off. I thought he was teasing me. He asked to share his experience with the group. I recognized him as the guest who kept laughing and making fun of me earlier in the tour, but I let him share his story anyhow. It could be fun to hear what he had cooked up for us.

He said that after the group left the room, he and his wife stayed behind so that she could take his photo while sitting on the old church pew which was next to the flashlight. He was laughing and telling her that I was full of baloney, and that he knew that there were no ghosts. He went on to say that he was going to prove to her that the ghost stories were faked.

He asked Eliza to turn off the flashlight if she really existed. As he sat on the pew with his arms crossed and a smirk on his face, the flashlight turned off. It had to be a coincidence so he asked her to turn it back on. It turned back on. He said he still didn't believe it, and so it flashed off and on repeatedly. This is the part where he screamed. By the time we got back into the room the flashing had stopped, making it appear that he had made the whole thing up.

He was begging us to believe him. He said that he is not crazy, that it really did turn off on command. He said that he was really very sorry for making fun of me, please believe him! He asked Eliza again, this time in front of us. Right on cue it turned off. The crowd shouted, some in surprise, some in fear. I had no explanation for them and was as surprised as everyone else. This was the first of many amazing experiences with the flashlight.

I should mention that my skeptical guest came back the next day to try to debunk the flashlight himself. He turned it all around and took the batteries out until he was convinced that I didn't make any of it up. He called me when he got home to New Jersey and apologized again for calling me names.

I would have to say that the experiment worked during about half of the tours from this point on, but only if I did it in the game room. I always shared the story about the skeptical man, and right when I get to the part where he is screaming it would sometimes start to flash as if on cue. Often times my guests would ask questions in hopes of prompting a response. I realized after a while that guests were asking the same basic questions over and over again and the flashlight was responding the same way each time. Over the next year I began to see a pattern with the answers that the flashlight provided.

Her real name is either Elizabeth, Rebecca or something like that. She is in her middle years and is a mother. She is Caucasian and was not a servant or slave, but was the lady of the house and in charge. She loves children, especially girls. She is not the only spirit in the house. She enjoys the tours and she considers herself to be my friend.

One time I forgot to bring batteries for the light, and so I simply set it down on the table and explained the experiment. A few minutes later a woman raised a shaking hand. She was looking rather flustered. She said that every time I described the flashlight turning off, she and the ladies on each side of her saw that their cell phones were turning off and on.

A few months later I heard from security that they came up to the game room at closing to asks some guests to exit the house. When he saw that they were trying to talk to Eliza, he and the guests tried to use his security flashlight to get a response, but were not able to get it to turn off or on. After a few minutes the guard glanced up into the foyer and noticed that the hallway chandelier was swinging back and forth. He thought it might be a minor earth tremor or something of that nature, but nothing else in the house was shaking or moving.

Once, a guest brought a smart phone on the tour that had this "ghost radar" and "spirit box" application on it. He said that he bought them for entertainment purposes only, but it actually seemed to be coming up with words and names that were valid throughout his vacation.

He set his phone down next to the flashlight. It had what looked like a Doppler radar on it. I watched a little dot go from green to red and approach the flashlight. It appeared as if it was standing right next to me when the flashlight turned on. I held my breath as we watched the dot move away from the table then approach from another angle. The flashlight turned off again. This went on for about 15 minutes. The flashlight turned off or on only when the dot turned from green to red and appeared to approach the table.

On Wednesday, September 22, 2010, Vicky was hosting an evening tour for about 20 some guests. When they got into the game room she first told them about the flashlight experiment, then she set the flashlight on the table and offered the guests to come back after the tour and try it with their own flashlights.

Much to her surprise a guest pulled an identical flashlight out of his pocket and asked if he could try it then. She set both flashlights together on the table. Just as she set the new flashlight down the first flashlight turned off. She jokingly told Eliza that she was supposed to turn both off at the same time. At this moment they both started to go off, however as one turned on the other turned off.

Vicky, the true showman that she was, teased Eliza by saying, "No no no, you got it all wrong. You have to turn them both off at the exact same time!"

The audience watched in amazement as both flashlights started to turn off and on in sync. This to me seemed to validate the claim that the flashlight phenomenon is not mechanical, but Vicky remained unconvinced. If it was mechanical, I argued, how could both lights flicker in perfect unison? Vicky had no explanation.

Orb floating over the flashlight table, 2011

Cameras and Orbs

We already talked about the idea that entities can gain energy from the energy that we humans emit, but did you know that they can also become stronger from taking the energy from our electronic equipment?

On March 25, 2010, I had a group of around 30 people attending the tour. This was one of my earliest tours, and so I was still permitted to bring guests down into the basement. As we entered the basement some of the guests began to mumble that they didn't like it down there. Everyone seemed very nervous and several people left and waited for me in the garden.

Photo of the basement taken while on a ghost tour.
Some people think that they see faces or shadows in this photo. 2010

Most visitors bring digital or video cameras with them on the tour. I encourage them to take photos and to email the strange ones to me to share on future tours. As the guests attempted to take photos, many of the cameras suddenly lost power. Some of the guests said that the batteries, which were fresh, had suddenly died.

One man said that his very expensive and reliable camera was malfunctioning for the first time ever. Another woman said that the memory was full, even though she had just emptied it before the tour. By the time we were ready to go back into the house the cameras were all back in working order. This was the first of many odd occurrences that guests received when using their cameras in the house.

Williamsburg Paranormal Society, Photo by Shelley Thacker Millirons, 2008

Strange behavior from our cameras became so common that I actually stopped making notes in my journal when they happened. I did however make note of one very strange occurrence that resulted in a ghostly image caught on a cell phone camera on April 29, 2010.

Hazel attended a morning tour, but unfortunately she forgot her camera. After the tour was over she stood by the front door and said a proper goodbye to Eliza, curtsying in the traditional colonial style. She told the ghost that she would be greatly honored if she could have some sort of confirmation of the presence of the lady of the house, then she promised to return with her camera.

Later in the evening she and her husband returned to the house with her digital camera which had just been fully charged. They asked another couple to take their photo posing in front of the house, but when the couple handed the camera back it was dead. Hazel felt sure that this was a sign that Eliza was standing nearby.

Cell phone photo of mist figure in front of the fire place in the pink room.
Photo by Hazel, 2010

Her husband refused to enter the house, so brave Hazel entered the empty house alone. As she was standing in front of the fireplace in the pink room she suddenly remembered that her new cell phone had a camera on it, although Hazel had never used it before. She took a photo of the fireplace and glanced at the phone to see if it worked. She was amazed to see a very clear mist figure standing in front of the fireplace. The entire center of the photo was blurred, however the edges were clear. If you look carefully you can see what seems to be a shadow of a head and shoulders in the center of the mist. Some people think that it could be a shadow of two people standing next to each other.

I know what you're thinking. You are thinking that Hazel altered the photo on Photoshop right? I would be tempted to think that Hazel added in the mist before emailing the photo to me; however Hazel mentioned that she showed it to Caleb shortly after taking the photo, and so I did a little investigating.

I asked the guard if he remembered the photo as it appeared that day on Hazel's phone. He looked at the image that she emailed to me and said that it was identical to the image he saw on her phone that day. The mist figure photo was definitely not altered, or embellished on Photoshop

A Playful Orb Visits the Front Gate

I should mention that many of our guests get very excited when they take a photo that shows an orb floating in it. Please keep in mind that just because you captured an orb in your photo does not mean that a location is haunted. There are many definitions and theories about ghost orbs.

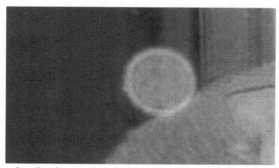
A rather impressive orb on a woman's shoulder, 2010

Most paranormal investigators define an orb as being the soul of a once living person that appears as a spherical shaped light. We cannot usually see these orbs with our own eyes, but they can be captured on film.

Some investigators discredit photos with orbs, claiming that the camera is just picking up the reflection of dust particles, moisture or an insect. I have countless photos of the Manor

House with big and little orbs. I have no idea if they are paranormal or just an insect, so I have included many of them in this book for you to look at and decide for yourself.

One quiet afternoon I was scheduled to work at the Recreation desk. I was hoping for something exciting to happen, since working there meant that I was mostly folding towels and shooing kids out of the hot tubs. This security guard, who I had not met before, came down to tell me a story.

October was unusually cold in 2012, and many mornings we would wake to find ice or frost on our car windows. The night of the front gate mystery was no exception, and the security team were bundled in their jackets trying to keep warm inside of their small shack.

The midnight shift was passing the time by watching the many video monitors that are stationed up at the front Gate. One young man noticed an odd shape floating between the gate and the fence near the front of the resort on his monitor. He poked his head out of the building to see if he could see any sort of bug or bird that could be making this odd shape on the screen but the night was very still since it was unusually cold. It was far too cold for any large bug to be flying in the night air.

He returned to his station and watched mesmerized as the orb floated between the shack and the front entrance. As it neared the camera he guessed that it was about the size of a tennis ball. He could see no evidence of wings that you might see on a bat or a bird. Every few minutes he poked his head out to see if he could figure out what it was, but he never saw or heard anything odd with his own eyes. Only the camera could capture the image.

This bizarre orb continued to slowly meander between the gate and the shack on the video for at least 10 more minutes. He eventually recorded it on his cell phone so that he could show his coworkers. When the rest of the team saw the video they were as puzzled as the guy who witnessed it. They have never seen anything like this before and have not seen anything like it since.

Tours Attract Psychics

As you can imagine, the ghost tours are a magnet for some very interesting people. Several times a month a guest will often approach me and tell me that they are psychic, able to see ghosts, or their great grandmother on their father's side was able to speak to the dead.

I certainly believe that there are gifted psychics out there, but I had no idea that so many people had this ability until I started meeting them on my tours. The first experience I had with a psychic was on one of my earliest tours. This was long before I posted the journal on Facebook, or offered to send e-mails out to guests with the stories. It was almost as if she had taken the tour before and was quoting me, but I knew we had never met.

She was a lovely older lady who said that she was part of a ghost investigative team, and that she came on the tour because she was curious if her interpretations would match my stories. She wanted to tell me her visions before the tour, so I pulled her to the side and asked her to tell me what she saw. She said some very exciting things

She went into detail about the hateful prisoner, and the piles of dead men in the basement. On the first floor she saw the surgical operations being done and the strict man lurking by the front door, trying to shoo us out. She could even smell his cigar smoke in the house. She said that there was a lady who was very loving and sweet, but was also in charge of the house.

She fully described Eliza's physical appearance as I described her earlier. This was the first time that I had heard this from a psychic and so I was quite shocked. She said that Eliza was standing right next to us at that moment. As she said this we both felt a cold sensation and the hair on our arms stood up. Her husband gasped. It was uncanny.

Since this first experience I have had many sensitive people approach me with their interpretations. Some of them can see things. Some can feel things, smell things, or just know things. Most of them are adults, but I have had several children who see things too. Even babies have been observed staring and pointing at corners, as if there is something there. The unusual thing is that since I conduct most of the tours I get to hear all of their interpretations, and make note of them for comparison. After a while I could see that they all described roughly the same things and the same characters

Oh, I know exactly what you skeptics are thinking. You're sitting there with your arms crossed and mumbling that people are just repeating what they read in my journals. It is true that as I began posting my stories for the public that some people could have been influenced by what they read, but in the first six months there was no explanation for the similarities. My journals were not published or posted anywhere at that time.

Many of these people said that they have guides who give them information. A guide is sort of like a guardian angel. For some of these sensitive people, the guides were loved ones who have passed away but choose to keep in touch from beyond. A few of them said that their guide was a loved one who they knew from a past life, and assists them in this new life as a friend. I always knew that I had a guide with me since I was a young child. He guided my hand when I painted. I honestly didn't give it much thought, but just accepted it as normal for a visual artist. I didn't realize until recently that this was quite common with people of all talents..

Some of the psychic guests just simply saw things that the rest of us could not. The most fascinating experience was when the psychic from T.H.O.R. came to visit in advance of the team's investigation. Lucy repeated everything that this first psychic told me months earlier, but she also saw other things that I don't usually talk about on the tours, or even with friends.

She walked past the back of the house and placed her small hands to the left of the back door. She said that she smelled cooking. She said that this is where they prepared food. I corrected her and told her that meals were prepared in the building next to the house, but she shook her head insisting that she was right. It wasn't until later that night that I remembered that Iris once told me that there were the remains of an old stove pipe in the music room. This was the room that the Slauson family turned into their kitchen for a few years during the mid-20th century. This is the room Lucy smelled the yummy odors. Mrs. Slauson must have been a good cook.

The Psychic Lucy In the basement. She felt something horrible down there.

She also walked over to the Gazebo and said that she saw a big party with food and dancing. I never told her, and it is not widely known, that we rent the house and Gazebo out for weddings and large private parties

Lucy also saw many arrows on the hill near the tomb stone. She even went so far as to say a few gossipy things about a couple of my coworkers that I later found out to be true! Remind to never try to keep a secret from my friend Lucy.

Doors that Mysteriously Open

I must admit that it is tempting to lead people on when it comes to the paranormal experiences in the house, but I made a promise to Iris, and to myself, that I would keep the tours genuine. For this reason I am quick to tell folks that the hutch phenomenon is not paranormal.

What happens with the hutch is that when a large group of people enter the dining room, the old wooden floors, which date back to the Civil War era, sag with the weight of people. This causes the hutch to lean forward and the doors to pop open. I have seen it time and time again. I expect it to happen when we have a lot of people in that room, and it never ceases to make me giggle.

There have been a few times however, that it seems to happen without any physical explanation. Sometimes they open when I only have one visitor with me, and we are on the other side of the room. Sometimes they open when we are not even in the room, but can see them swing open from across the hall. Sometimes the room is full, but we have been standing still for several minutes, then the doors open right when I say something about Eliza.

They also seem to open for men who claim that they are skeptical, but not for men who are asking for it to open, regardless of their weight. When this happens the man is often walking around the corner, not looking where he is going, and the door will pop right in front of his face and startle him. When this happens it is actually quite funny, at least for me. One time however, it wasn't funny when it happened to me. I am sure that Eliza enjoyed making me screech and jump out of my shoes.

Usually when they open, they bang open several times in a row, but then we cannot get them to open again without using great force. When this happens I ask someone to dance a jig in front of the hutch to try to open it without touching it. Of course this brings howls of laughter from the group but nothing short of physically prying the doors open with your hands will open them up again if the "ghost" opens them first.

My first manager, Belinda, swears that when she was hosting murder mystery tours in the room that it would always open as she was giving introductions, even though everyone was sitting still. She would then introduce Eliza and then the doors of the hutch would just sort of open as if pulled by an unseen hand. She said that this happened almost every single time they had this event. Iris also did the murder mystery tours in the same room, and it happened often for her as well.

Is it a ghost or is it gravity? I guess I will never know, and so I will let you decide for yourself. Just remember that when something unexpected like this happens when you are on a ghost tour, it is important to remain calm and always think logically before jumping to the conclusion that you have just witnessed something paranormal.

During spring break of 2011 I had a huge crowd for a mid-day tour. It was one of those rowdy, uppity groups who like to joke and tease, and so there was a lot of energy in the house that day. After a flashlight session I told the group that it was time to move into the next room. Since I was crowded into the back of the game room and I could not lead the group out, so I asked them to go ahead without me.

After a few minutes I realized that no one was moving from the foyer. I made my way through the crowd to see what was going on and asked why they didn't go into the library. One guest standing near the room said that the door was closed, and they didn't know if they were allowed to go in. I said that it was OK, that the ghosts don't mind, or something sarcastic like that, and much to everyone's astonishment the library door swung opened on its own. Of course I figured that it was a guest playing a joke on us, however the room was empty. There were several people who refused to enter the room

Usually when I give a tour I like to arrive at least 30 minutes early so that I can check the house and sit and rest for a few minutes. This particular spring afternoon I was sitting right in front of the entry way, listening to the sound of my first guests approaching the house. I looked up just as the front door opened as if pulled by an invisible hand. A young boy stood at the bottom of the stairs, staring at me wide eyed with his mouth agape. He shouted, "Wow, look mom, the ghosts opened the door for me! Cool!" He marched right into the house as excited as if he was going to a party at Chucky Cheeses.

One afternoon in early summer of 2011, I was standing with my back to the Pink Room, and as usual the door was open behind me. I greeted the group of about 20 guests and told them that I was very excited to be with them that day, and if we were lucky we might see some sort of activity.

At this very moment the door behind me shut rather loudly, bumping me on my backside and causing me to leap into the air. I opened it again to see who had interrupted me, however the room was empty. My group thought I had rigged it to close like that, but I allowed them to investigate the door and they found nothing hooked up to it to make it close on command. They were quite impressed as was I. I must say however that I do not appreciate being bumped on my backside. I wish that the ghosts would stop doing that. I am sure that they find this activity to be quite amusing.

T.H.O.R. all felt cold spots then their equipment went off.
Emily Christoff Flowers, 2010

Chapter Eleven

Paranormal Investigators and Their Gadgets

Did you know that ghost hunting goes well back into ancient history? More recently there was a rich and well documented period of time in the United States and Europe which is referred to as the spiritualist movement. It lasted from 1848 until the mid-1930s. This movement is defined as a loose set of faith based beliefs and practices that related to the attempted communication between the living and the dead. Individuals worked to either prove or disprove the existence of the afterlife through the use of dowsing rods, séances, voice recordings and photography.

At the time of around the Civil War, over 10% of Americans practiced the art of communicating with the dead. Primarily their efforts were an entertaining diversion to pass the long winter nights, however many people reached great fame through their abilities. Unfortunately some well-paid mediums were eventually discovered to be fraudulent, and so respect for the spiritualists eventually came to a screeching halt. Modern day paranormal investigators fight these pre-conceived prejudices against them on a daily basis today, however this does not deter them from creating new and effective ways of attempting to validate the existence of spirits. (Schill)

There is a legend that Thomas Edison himself had attempted to create his own ghost voice box in an effort to prove that science could verify all unexplainable, paranormal events. Earliest actual ghost recordings were made after Edison's death, on a magnetophone, by Italian Monks, in 1943. Modern day ghost hunters use electric magnetic field detectors, cameras, thermometers, dowsing rods and all sorts of other fun gadgets to attempt communication with the other side. (Watson)

When we record these voices on a digital recorder, computer, telephone or video camera they are referred to as Instrumental Trans Communication, or ITC. When you catch these voices, specifically on a recorder, it is defined as Electronic Voice Phenomenon, or EVP.

I had heard about the effects of EVPs, but I of course was a non-believer. I figured that it was most likely the interference of radios or maybe even a baby monitor that people were picking up on their recorders. I assumed that many of the ghost hunting reality shows contrived the results of the ghost voices. As a result of my own prejudices I was not prepared for the EVPs captured in the house during paranormal investigations. They were in direct response to questions or statements made by us living humans, as if the ghosts were talking back to us.

I have yet to read a clear description of what exactly causes an EVP. Some argue that ghosts use the sound waves from our voices to produce the sound that they need to record their own voices. Others suggest that ghosts use a much higher shift in frequency than living people, making it impossible to hear with your own ears, but possible to hear after it is played back at full volume and a different speed on a computer. Whichever the case may be, our house seems to be a great place to record the voices of ghosts.

Voices of Spirits Caught

I should mention that most requests by professional paranormal investigation groups to hunt for ghosts in the house are declined by our big wigs. I have been told that it is for fear of raising paranoia with our guests, or concern that we would attract a "bunch of wackos". This one big wig actually said this to my face! I laughed when he told me this, and reminded him that I was one of those wackos. He didn't think it was funny. The more I think about it, the more I realize that I am very lucky to still have a job.

Did you know that at the time that the house was built, that most men wore wigs? If you were poor your wig was made out of horse hair and it would rub your neck raw, so you were called a "red neck". If you were the middle sort your wig was made from goat hair, so you were called an "Old Goat". The really important dudes showed off their wealth by having huge wigs made of very expensive human hair. They were usually the ones in charge. They were called the "Big Wigs".

Anyhow, the only reason that Williamsburg Paranormal Society, and Toledo Haunted Occurrences Research, were allowed to conduct their experiments was because one of the members of the groups were friends with employees of the resort, who vouched for their professionalism. Hopefully this attitude will change as the world becomes more accepting of paranormal research. Maybe "wacko" will become the new norm.

Toledo Haunted Occurrences Research team members responded
to a loud knocking sound on the second floor of the Kitchen Restaurant.
Emily Christoff Flowers, 2010

Fortunately, our local ghost hunters had the luck of being able to investigate the house overnight a number of times in an attempt to find EVPs. Williamsburg Paranormal Society's first EVP encounter was on January 24, 2008, very late at night.

Iris told me that two male investigators were in the third floor former art studio. They were having some difficulty walking around due to the amount of boxes being stored in the room at the time. One investigator said to the other, "There is a lot of stuff in this room!" At the time they said this they did not hear any female voices, but later they heard the recording of a woman's voice softly whisper in response, "I'm Sorry."

I thought this story was fascinating, but I suspected Iris of teasing me when she told me about it, so I begged her to give me the phone number of the woman in charge of WPS. I had never met a real life ghost hunter at this time, so I was unsure of what to expect.

I must say that Shelley is fearless. I can't imagine having the guts to sneak around a haunted house for a living. Ok, yeah, I know that I sneak around a haunted house for a living, but she does it in houses and places that she is not familiar with. For some reason that seems a bit more dangerous to me.

Anyhow, Shelley and her team have investigated countless hotels, graveyards and homes in Williamsburg and have a great track record of finding evidence of the spirit world. Shelley is also a professional photographer, and so she has caught some incredible images on film. She tackles her investigations with gusto, so you can imagine my shock when she confided to me that she was scared to death to be alone in the game room on the second floor of the manor house. She said that it just didn't feel right to her and that she had a very bad experience there on one of her investigations.

The night of this experience the house had all of the lights turned off as usual, and it was some ungodly hour. Shelly's team was taking turns entering the house in pairs while the other members waited outside. Shelley was with another investigator on the second floor foyer. She went into the game room and sat down in the center of the loveseat, assuming that her coworker was following right behind. When she discovered that the other investigator had not joined her, Shelley shouted out, "Don't you leave me in this room by myself!"

Our investigator had two digital recorders. One recorder caught the response, "Oh OK." The second one caught, "Oh, Ok, slide over silly girl."

Apparently Shelley was taking up too much space on the two person loveseat, and the ghost couldn't fit on the couch next to her. Eliza just wanted to keep poor Shelley company.

Later that night one of the investigators asked another team member if they were allowed to go up to the third floor. They did not hear any other voices at the time, but when they got home and listened to the recordings on their computer you could clearly hear a man's voice say, "Alright." A few minutes later he said, "Door open, come on in." Then it exclaimed, "So Awesome." Iris had left the studio door unlocked for the group and the spirits were telling them to come on in.

Shelley thought this was very strange that a ghost from another time would use the currently popular phrase, "awesome". Was our ghost the spirit of a skater kid who got caught in the house?

Shelley was very perplexed and so she did a little investigation and discovered that the word awesome was a very common exclamation during colonial times. The word meant something different however to the colonists than it means to us today. Awesome meant to be afraid, in grief, pain and dread, just as the word was used in the Bible. It is not the funny slang word that my kids use today when they find out that they actually passed their calculus class.

One very simple trick that you can do on your own, if you suspect that your home may be haunted, is to just knock on a table and ask the ghost to repeat the knock. One night in 2008 the Williamsburg Paranormal Society was conducting an investigation at the house and caught a very fascinating EVP of a ghost knocking.

On the recording you can hear the investigator knock 3 times and ask Eliza to knock back. According to Shelley he was standing on the second floor in the foyer facing the game room. After about 30 seconds of silence he heard three distinct knocks come from the area of the game table. He knocked again, and again it was repeated. When Shelley told me this I was skeptical, however after hearing the recording myself I thought this was very cool.

Shelley is sitting on the love seat where she later heard an EVP asking her to slide over.   Williamsburg Paranormal Society, 2009

A few years later when T.H.O.R. investigated they caught several EVPs of knocking sounds and the sounds of footsteps coming from the empty third floor studio. They also caught a breathy sound of something saying the word "no', and a sigh, also from the unoccupied studio.

One EVP from T.H.O.R. knocked my socks off. It was recorded in the game room, sitting next to the flashlight. Someone asked who the ghosts were. It responded with, "We are the sleepers, unknown."

You can hear this EVP on their web site at www.thorparanormal.com. (Sayer) I wonder if the word "sleepers" was another way to say, "dead people".

Ghost Box

Two members of the paranormal investigative team, called Supernatural Anomalies Investigations, or SAI, came to the resort in the fall of 2010, to see if they could get permission to do a full investigation of the house. I should explain that they had never heard of the manor house before this time, since they were from out of state, and so they were not familiar with any of the stories. They said that they were just driving by, saw that it was an old plantation house, and thought they would just check it out.

Unfortunately I was not able to get permission for them to do a full overnight investigation, but I was able to take Dan and Shawn through the house for a quick casual impromptu tour in the afternoon. I was curious to see all of their interesting equipment, and I must admit that I was thrilled when they pulled out their "Ghost Box".

I had heard of these contraptions, but had never seen a real one in person. Basically it is a small portable radio that has been altered so that it continuously scans the radio waves. When it is on it creates audio remnants and white noise from broadcast stations. The idea is that ghosts are able to manipulate this frequency into words and sentences in an attempt to communicate with the living. I was highly disbelieving that the box worked since it seemed so easy to fake the results on those TV reality shows. I told the guys my thoughts on this, and they actually agreed. They just bought the thing and were curious to see if it really worked.

Dan put the headphones on and Shawn explained that Dan could no longer participate in our conversation. He could only hear the white noise and music coming from the box. It was turned up so loudly that I could actually hear it from across the room. Shawn said that Dan would repeat every word out loud that he could hear come through the static, but that he could not hear us and so his words would make no sense to us.

As soon as we walked into the blue room, the box said "home". This made me feel pretty good since I feel very much like I am home when I am in the house, but I was sure that it was just a coincidence at the time. I was still convinced that there is no way that a ghost can talk through a radio.

At this moment the front door opened and a guest walked into the house and interrupted us. I soon realized that this man had been drinking and was hiding something naughty behind his back. He slurred, "I want to see Lizeeeeeee! I'm here to catch me a ghost". At this point the ghost box said, "Searching". He swayed as he spoke, then giggled and burped. I was not amused.

After a failed attempt to explain that there was no tour that day, I saw that the drunkard had the nerve to be hiding a lit cigar behind his back. Did he really think that I wouldn't smell it or see the smoke? I was livid, but I kept my smile as I explained to him that he had to remove the cigar from the house. He just stood there smiling at me and scratching his bald head. Obviously he couldn't understand me. I took a deep calming breath and spoke very slowly as I often did with my kids when they were young. "Sir, the ghosts do not like lit cigars in their home. This makes them mad." The man turned pale and staggered quickly out the door again.

Shawn asked me what the words "get out" meant. I was confused because I did not hear the ghost box say this. I just said something about the strict man telling offensive people to get out. I wasn't totally sure I heard him right. Later, as I watched their video, I clearly saw and heard the entire incident. I was stunned that the strict man had communicated through the box just as this rude man walked in the door.

When I took a very close look at the video I could also see a flicker of what looked like a black cloak or perhaps a dark shadow of a very short person or child run past the door right after the man left. At the time that this man was in the house with us, we were the only other people present. In the video you can't hear footsteps of anyone walking in the foyer. If you go to www.supernaturalai.com, you can see it on the video ending in number 844, at exactly 05:48 minutes into the video. If you pause the video, you can even see a very clear shadow. Please ignore the horrible oversized uniform I was wearing and the fact that I was having a very bad hair day.

The ghost box continued to amaze me as I walked with them through the house. At one time it said "first names", and I introduced the men. Then it said, "hers". I was confused and said that Eliza should know me, I am Em. Later it said "Elizabeth, and then I realized that she was trying to tell me that her proper name was Elizabeth.

As we moved through the house I told Shawn that I would tell them as many of the stories as I had time for, and see if the ghosts responded as they often did during our tours. At this point the box said, "Stories, all of them." The men were as amazed as I was. Well, OK, you want me to tell all of the stories? I do love to talk, so what the heck, why not?

When we got upstairs to the dining room the box became very active. Dan said that it was giving him garbled words which he said made no sense to him. It said, "Water, leaving us," and "Ohio". He asked if this made any sense to me.

I felt the blood drain from my face. This was impossible. No one at work knew at this time that I was considering moving back to my home state of Ohio. These two guys could not even know that I came from Ohio, since it is not something that I discuss on tours or mention on a regular basis. I hadn't even posted my wish to move on Facebook or my blog yet, but my family and I were hoping to move to a small town located on the banks of the great Maumee River, and I was having a hard time deciding whether to do this now or wait for a few more years until my youngest was out of school.

Was this just an amazing coincidence? How could these men know this when even my own boss had yet to find out? As I thought about it I remembered that I had several phone conversations with my parents about our move while I thought that I was alone in the house. I also remembered talking about it with my friend Lucy during her visit with T.H.O.R. I think that the ghosts overheard me and they knew that I was considering leaving them soon.

When we entered the game room I set the flashlight on the table and it started to turn off and on for them right away as I continued my stories. I told them that I hoped that Eliza didn't feel like a trick pony, and then I explained to them that Eliza likes to play with the flashlight. I told them that I didn't know why she had such a fascination with it, and the ghost box said, "Toy". Eliza thinks the flashlight is a toy, how funny.

I suspect that both investigators left the house amazed. (Taylor)

A mist appears on the right side of this photo, as Shelley and her team members search for ghosts. Williamsburg Paranormal Society, 2009

Taunting the Monster

I was quite surprised when I received permission for Toledo Haunted Occurrences Research to come down from Ohio for a 3 day investigation in mid-July of 2010. I was already friends with their psychic Lucy, since she went to school with my sisters and we shared many mutual friends. Lucy loved reading my stories by e-mail and so she and the team made the trip down to check it out.

T.H.O.R. is a team of highly trained professionals and is quite well known and respected in northern Ohio. Ross and Bryan lead the group. They were accompanied by Becky, who was handling the videos. Lucy, and her husband, also a trained meta-physicist joined in for the visit.

I had the incredible honor of being invited along for their overnight investigation, and was able to see how they use their equipment to record and test odd paranormal phenomenon. It took them about an hour to set up everything. I felt like I was on an episode of the television show "Ghost Hunters", as we turned off all of the lights and began wandering around in the pitch blackness of the house with our cameras, KII meters and digital recorders.

One of the reasons I was so excited about T.H.O.R.'s visit was because I wanted them to find an explanation for a number of the more unusual occurrences, especially the shadow figures and the flashlight.

The unique thing about the group is that there primary objective is to prove that what we are experiencing can be explained by science. They are not looking for ghosts, they are looking to debunk and explain our paranormal activity. When T.H.O.R. claims that a home is haunted, it is only because they have ruled out all other explanations for the paranormal phenomenon.

The night of the investigation was a sweltering 85 degrees after dark, and the air conditioning in the house was broken of course. At first I thought this was a horrible thing, but I found out later that it was much easier to detect ghosts in the heat.

As Bryan approached the stairs leading up to the second floor his KII started to react and he shouted for the rest of us to join him on the landing between the stairs. We all stood there in amazement as the various instruments were going off and we felt cold pockets of air winding between us. There was no possible way that we were feeling the air conditioning, but just to make sure Ross reached up and felt the vent. It was blowing hot air. I started snapping photos.

An odd photo in the basement of the Kitchen Restaurant, taken during an investigation. Emily Christoff Flowers, 2010

At this time I took a photo from the bottom of the stairs looking towards two of the team members who were standing by the front door. My Camera's flash suddenly stopped working so I decided to take the photo using only the light of my small flashlight. There was absolutely no other light source in the room at the time. The next day when I lightened this photo up as much as possible, I could clearly see a dark shadow standing to the left of the front table. The shadow was shaped like a large man, but it did not wrap around the contours of the table like a normal shadow. It seemed to be formed somehow in front of me, and was standing up straight in the middle of the room next to Lucy and her husband. There is no way that this shadow could be from them since the only light source in the room came from my right hand. I did not realize at the time that I took this photo that my quiet, predictable life was about to change drastically.

A photo taken during an investigation showing what appears to be a shadow figure to the right of the investigators. Notice how it seems to be in front of the table.
Emily Christoff Flowers, 2010

Lucy felt that she was being grabbed, poked and prodded by unseen hands, and that it was trying to urge us up to the second floor, so we all pushed our way past the cold spots and filed into the game room where the flashlight was waiting for us.

As we cautiously entered the dark room, everything seemed very quiet at first. The only sound you could hear was our labored breathing in the heat as we circled the table. Just as I asked Eliza to communicate with us, the flashlight immediately responded and the team's equipment started flashing. We could also feel a pocket of cold air near the flashlight. The men were ecstatic!

Later Ross, Bryan and Becky crouched next to the light as Lucy and I watched them from downstairs on the video monitors. They tried placing the light in different areas around the room, but it only seemed to work on the table. My own flashlight, which was identical to the one upstairs, was sitting next to me beside the monitors. I decided to ask Eliza if she could turn mine off too, not expecting her to respond to a different flashlight in a different part of the house. Lucy and I gasped as it obediently turned off. For several minutes they blinked off and on in sync.

We had cold drinks and food on the third floor when we needed to take a break. There were a few occasions where Bryan was sitting quietly in the studio and he heard footsteps approaching up the stairs. He ran over to the door and opened it, but as expected the narrow winding stairs were empty. He was unable to capture this on video, but this personal experience had him very puzzled, and he could find no explanation for it. I was glad that he had validated my own experiences. Later, as I mentioned earlier, they realized that they caught several EVPs from this room throughout the night.

We were nearing exhaustion by 2:00 am; however we wanted to take a quick walk through the Kitchen Restaurant. Charles keyed us in and stood patiently waiting by the front door. The dining room looked very different after dark and with all of the lights off. First Lucy and I walked upstairs. The second floor is just a small intimate dining room with a bathroom off of the hall. She said that she felt nothing out of place there and her equipment was blank, so we came back down.

For the next twenty minutes or so the team walked through the three floors of the small building, hoping to find some evidence, but the kitchen was hushed under a blanket of silence.

Just as the team announced that they were leaving, Charles heard a very clear knocking sound coming from the empty second floor dining room. He paused and looked at me out of the corner of his eye, "Did you just hear that?"

I did! We shouted for the group to come back and check it out. They scurried back into the room, cameras in hand. When Lucy hit the stairs she exploded in an earsplitting scream

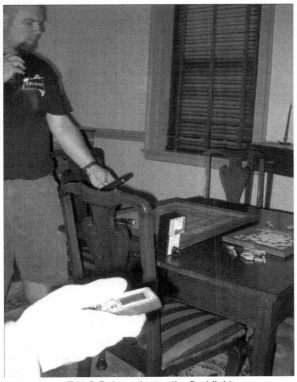

T.H.O.R. investigates the flashlight,
Emily Christoff Flowers, 2010

She gasped that it was the strongest paranormal sensation that she has felt all night. It was there on the stairs and it was grabbing her. Bryan and Ross ran up protectively behind her. Their equipment started to spike. Something was prowling there.

I chose this moment to take a photo of the main dining room. Later I realized that I had captured what appeared to be a mist or blurry shape in the center of the room. I guess the ghost of the kitchen did not want us to leave until he made himself known.

A misty form in the Kitchen Restaurant.
Emily Christoff Flowers, 2010

The kitchen revived us and so we made one final trip down to the basement. I had been dreading this all night. I had to muster up all of my courage when they finally decided that we would take the plunge into full dark and have me turn off all of the lights down there. I reluctantly made my way up the wooden staircase to reach the last power switch. I hate these stairs, as they sway and creak when you walk on them. My hands were shaking as my fingers pressed the light switch and we were thrown into total darkness.

It felt like we were surrounded by a thick black soup that seemed to come alive with moving shadows. I carefully made my way back down the old stairs by feeling the cracked brick wall next to me and by following the shouts of the team. I could feel the soft touch of cobwebs pulling at my hair as my eyes adjusted to the gloom. The old boxwood shrubs covering the windows filtered the moonlight into the room, which caused flickering shadows every time the wind would play with the branches.

At the bottom of the stairs is this wooden storage closet. You can see through the slits of the wood well enough to make out fleeting shadows and bright reflections from the wine bottles stored inside. It always seemed to me that something was hiding in the dark secretive space, and I could imagine that the fingers of a decrepit soul could just fit in between the slats as he tried to claw his way out.

The team wanted to tease the evil man out of hiding by shouting names at him and provoking him. I knew that this is common practice for many ghost hunters, and is done to get some sort of evidence, but a little voice inside my head said not to participate. I was afraid that he would become angry and perhaps hurt one of us. But I guess I wanted to impress the group, so I gave my reluctant approval. Peer pressure stinks, even as a grown up.

"You're a coward", screamed Bryan at the ghost.

Ross banged the side of the storage closet and taunted, "Come out and talk to us, and make yourself known!"

We teased him for pinching children, called him an evil freak, and urged him to come out and fight like a man.

As we were provoking the monster, Lucy screamed and said that something had jumped on her back. She was able to shake it off eventually but we were both pretty upset. Let me tell you, you don't know fear until you stand next to a screaming psychic, in the middle of a totally black haunted basement, filled with squirmy things and angry ghosts.

I was hardly able to breathe. Lucy, who was trembling next to me and clutching my arm, kept sobbing that something was still trying to grab and poke her. I kept thinking that I saw it crouched in the shadows and looking at us with its black penetrating gaze through the slits of the wine closet. It was too horrible. We had to go back outside. Lucy and I ran out together, clutching at each other in fear.

We took many photos, EVP recordings and video footage in hopes of capturing this evil ghost, but much to my dismay the equipment picked up nothing from the depths of the cellar. I thought that my encounter with the prisoner was all over. Little did I know how wrong I was.

After we crawled out of the basement, the exhausted team loaded up their cars with all of the equipment, and went back into the house one last time to thank Eliza for her hospitality.

A few days after the tour, my assistant Vicky was doing her usual flashlight questions and asked it if Eliza enjoyed her visit with T.H.O.R. It lit up bright and strong.

The morning after the investigation I was exhausted but euphoric. It was the oddest sensation, and I contributed it to lack of sleep. I have heard that ghost hunting can cause this high sensation the next day, but I did not expect to feel that great. I was also very excited that we had proven that the ghosts in the mansion really do exist. I could hardly contain myself.

That night however I started to feel very unwell. By The next day I was ill and remained feeling sick for about a month. It wasn't as if I had a physical illness, it was something mental, as if I wasn't quite myself.

For the next month I had difficulty sleeping and constant nightmares when I did. My family and co-workers noticed a change in my behavior as well. I was an anxious mess even though my life was happy and predictable. These and other symptoms which I don't even want to mention became so severe that I eventually visited my doctor who pronounced me as being very healthy, and suggested a new line of work or at least a vacation. She diagnosed me as experiencing work related anxiety.

My friend Lucy had another idea though. She didn't think that my illness was physical; she thought that I was feeling the effects of the bad ghost from the basement. She thought that when that thing clung to her back that it also clung to mine. She was able to shake it off that night, but since I didn't have her psychic sensitivities I didn't realize that it had sort of stuck with me like some kind of invisible leech. She did not believe that it was demonic, just an angry ghost. She said that this was quite common for paranormal investigators to experience this, and that I needed to learn to protect myself in the future.

Lucy gave me a list of things to do to get back to normal. After several weeks of meditation, exercise, prayer and then finally a week of vacation to see my parents back in Ohio, it left as suddenly as it arrived. I also made sure that I apologized to the prisoner of the basement and assured him that I would never again take part in an interrogation of him, and if I had to go down there again that I would   do so with the utmost respect towards him.

By the time I finally got back in touch with Bryan and Ross in September, I had almost convinced myself that all I had experienced was just some sort of bizarre anxious reaction to their investigation. It all just seemed like the memory of a nightmare that started to go fuzzy over time.

I was sort of embarrassed to tell the men of my symptoms, since I thought for sure that they would think I was a brick shy of a full load, but Lucy thought that it might be important for them to know.

Lucy and I ware shocked when we learned that the two of them had the exact same symptoms as I had. It didn't last as long for them as it did for me however, but it was strong enough to cause them quite a lot of misery. Like me, they were reluctant to tell anyone about this until the symptoms had passed. They didn't even tell each other until weeks later.

It was surprising that T.H.O.R. didn't capture any evidence from the basement. They did however have many personal unexplainable things happen to them throughout the rest of the house. They got some great EVPs which I mentioned earlier, but the only thing that they captured on their video cameras was the flashlight phenomenon. They did feel however like the investigation was very informative, especially since the three of us shared the physical symptoms of being tormented by a negative entity. In their professional opinion the house is paranormally active. They also believe that the flashlight phenomenon is a genuine spirit event and would benefit from further investigation.

As you can imagine I am very reluctant to go back into the basement, but I felt very safe and healthy in the rest of the house, and had no fear of illness or of anything bad following me home. I continued to give sold out tours for a year after the investigation until they shut the house down for renovation in the spring of 2011.

I have not had any reoccurrence of this horrible entity participating in my life. I do make sure that I say a little prayer before entering the cellar, but strangely enough it feels almost as if he is gone from there now, or perhaps he is just content with my apology, and my more respectful attitude towards him.

Photo of Ross filming the storage area where people have seen the ghost of the prisoner of the basement.
Emily Christoff Flowers, 2010

I know that I learned one very important lesson from the investigation. As strange as it may sound to you, ghosts were people too. According to most theories, their personalities remain the same after death as they were in their life. They can experience anger, joy, sorrow and betrayal just as they did when they were human. One should not treat a spirit any differently than they would treat a living human being, and since it is not in my nature to bully or hurt people, I will never again taunt a ghost. Spirits must be treated with the same respect as the living.

Looking out the library window during the renovation.
When lightened, this photo showed two orbs and an odd shape or mist at the top left
of the window and top right corner. 2012

Chapter Twelve

My Last Thoughts on the Matter

For the next year after T.H.O.R.'s investigation I continued to be amazed during our tours. At the end of each one I begged my guests to mention the house in their comment cards. I hoped that the added attention that the house received through these curious visitors might draw the attention of our corporate office. We hoped that the big wigs would see that it desperately needed repairs, and that people cared.

The past owners of the resort had been promising to fix the house since before my first day of work, but the poor old thing was usually ignored for more pressing financial projects. It was falling down around us and we could do nothing about it. It is privately owned so we were not eligible for any sort of grant or government help.

Finally we were bought out by a larger, more compassionate company, and they saw the importance of the old home. I was thrilled when they announced that they were going to repair all of the water damage and peeling plaster. The majestic home would survive after all.

The Renovation

Once the restoration began on the house in June of 2011, we had to close it for a year. The repair was massive. In order to save the mansion they had to sand blast all of the old synthetic plaster and peeling paint from the inside of the house to let the porous brick dry out. Several new layers of organic plaster were applied. This new plaster was made from horse hair, crushed and fired oyster shells and some sort of animal fat. This is the same recipe that Richard Taliaferro used on his house in 1735.

Replacing the old windows with hand crafted glass
. Emily Christoff Flowers, 2012

They buried drains at the base of the foundation to wick the moister away into a nearby pond. Brand new windows were created using the same type of hand crafted glass that would have been installed in the 18th century. Special air-conditioning and heating units were installed that would keep the house safe and dry.

The basement had been renovated as well. They supported the massive hand hewn beams that remained from the Civil War era, filled in all of the holes in the floor and cleaned up the mess that had collected down there over the years.

I stopped by the house today to chit chat with the workers laying the new brick paths. I asked if they had any experiences in the house. One man said that he felt eyes on him in the basement. One other guy said that there is no way that he would ever set foot down there. They all looked at me like I was nuts. I should be getting used to this by now I guess.

Looking out at construction workers from the Music Room.
Emily Christoff Flowers, 2012

I was told that if I want to start bringing tours back into the basement when I start them up again in the summer of 2012 that I may, since it is now safe for guests to walk through. I shuddered when they told me this and said that I would think about it. That may take some convincing.

A photo of a worker renovating the basement.
Notice the small orb in on the left under the window.
Emily Christoff Flowers, 2012.

The Very Last of My Last Thoughts

Today, more people than ever are searching for ghosts. We have arrived at a wonderful time in history because of the popularity of the supernatural in our mainstream culture. It has become more acceptable in just the past few years for me to talk openly about my own experiences and for all of us to explore the notion of what really happens to us when we die, and that makes me very happy.

I still get a lot of doubters, so I try to explain it to people this way. If we were to go back in time to visit my Grandma Hazel and Grandpa Edwin on their little farm in Arlington Ohio during the great depression, they would welcome us with open arms. We would sit on their front porch and sip iced tea while we watched the sun set through their fields of corn.

We could try to tell them that in 2012 moving images would be transmitted into our homes from satellites which float above us in the atmosphere, but they would think we were mad. If we went on to explain that someday telephones will weigh only a few ounces, and can communicate with people from all over the world without using wires, and depend on a device the size of my thumbnail, they wouldn't believe us.

I can just picture Grandpa's puzzled face as he reacts to the news that humans will walk on the moon and then lose interest only a few years later. He would quietly chuckle when I tell him that one day we would clone a sheep named Dolly.

They might glance over at each other in a concerned way and say that this was impossible. They would say that science has discovered all that there is to discover in the great year of 1935, and so we must either be "put near gone", as Grandpa was fond of saying, or have very wild imaginations.

Grandma would then hand us a slice of homemade apple pie, and Grandpa would go back to milking his cows, shaking his head and laughing quietly. I wouldn't hate them for their disbelief; I would try to realize that this concept just doesn't fit into their world quite yet.

If I had my own way I would still have my head stuck in the sand myself I guess, refusing to accept a new way of looking at the world. I don't consider myself an overly brave person, but I do believe that it takes a bit of courage to accept a new direction in one's life and then to stand up for it against opposition. This takes much more courage than facing ghosts every day.

I still hesitate sometimes however when people ask me if the house is haunted, but not because I am embarrassed or fear for my job anymore. I pause because that word does not even begin to encompass everything that the manor house truly is.

I want people to understand that it is so much more than haunted. It has witnessed the rise and fall of the horrors of slavery, the destruction of the great Powhatan nation, and the birth of a new country. It survived the Civil War, and witnessed over 330 years of productive farming. It is not just a spooky old house; it is a historical gem with a personality all of its own. It is much more than just haunted. It is a living museum, deserving of recognition, love and respect.

It is not disrespectful though to tell the world that a historic home is haunted. There is absolutely nothing to be embarrassed about and no need to keep our ghosts a secret. Paranormal research is a highly respectful field, and we should be proud that our house is so active. Being haunted is not a thing of shame; it is a very special and exciting phenomenon.

Someday we will know what caused Eliza, Lydia, the Master, the Prisoner and Gus to linger in their home long after their physical death. Until that time I suggest that we all keep an open mind, and remember that at one time we were absolutely certain that the world was flat.

Manor house, Emily Christoff Flowers, 2012

About the Author

Emily Christoff Flowers graduated from Bowling Green State University in Ohio with her Bachelor's degree in Fine Art. For the next few decades she supported herself and her family by drawing portraits full time at amusement parks, malls, art shows and resorts. In 2012 she published her first children's book illustrations with author Carole Sarkan. The book is called, "And Candy Smiled" and will be available to purchase in June of 2012. She is currently illustrating Carol's next book, "Aunt Mary's Pottery".

Contact her, follow her continuing ghost adventures and find out how to meet Eliza in person at www.theghostjourmal.com. Follow our blog on Facebook at "Ghost Journals of a Haunted Manor House." Contact Emily at Emilychristoff@aol.com, and see her art portfolio at Emilychristoff.com.

Eiza standing next to Em during a tour.

A Big High Five

Thank you David, Halee, Eddie and James for cooking your own meals and vacuuming the living room while I worked two jobs. I have the deepest gratitude towards my beautiful daughter Halee for modeling for my painting on the front cover. Thanks again Iris, you're a great boss. Thanks to "Big Wigs" at the resort that have supported this project and given me your thumbs up over the years. A special thank you goes to Matthew for your love of the house, and for all of the research you have done over the years. Thank you also to Shelley for your beautiful photos. To all of you wonderful guests out there who have contributed stories and photos, a huge high five! Carole, you believed that I could write, and that means so much to me. Most of all, I love you Eliza for opening my eyes and for being my friend.

Bibliography

Adams, George W., (14 April, 2004), The National Historical Society's The Image of War: 1861-1865 Volume IV "*Fighting For Time*" < http://www.civilwarhome.com/medicinehistory.htm> February, 2012

Ancestry.com, Biographical Directory of the United States Congress, 1774 – 2005 (Provo,UT,USA, The Generations Network, Inc.,2006), www.ancestry.com, Database online. Record for Hamilton ward.

Balzano, Christopher, *Picture Yourself Ghost Hunting,* Course Technology PTR, 2009.

Bruton Parish, (2012), *A Brief History of Bruton Parish,* <http://www.brutonparish.org/history> March, 2012

Chadwick, Bruce, (11 December, 2008), The *Mysterious Death of Judge George Wythe,* Weider History Group at History.net, < http://www.historynet.com/the-mysterious-death-of-judge-george-wythe.htm> January, 2012

Cotton, Lee Pelham, (August 6, 2006), *Historic Jamestown – a Timeline for Structures at Jamestown, National Park Service,* < http://www.nps.gov/jame/historyculture/chiles-family-structures-timeline.htm> February, 2010

Daughters of the Golden West, (6 August, 2011), *Faces From The War Between the States,* <http://daughterofthegoldenwest.blogspot.com/2011/08/faces-from-war-between-states.html>

Elmore, Cindy, *Old Plantation Undergoing Time-Share Transformation*, Daily Press, Sunday, August 6th, 1984, Page G1

Friends of Green Spring, (2011*) Friends of the National Park Service for Green Spring, Inc.,* <http://www.historicgreenspring.org/> January, 2012

Hudson, Carson, (Summer 2000), *Occupied Williamsburg in the War Between the States.* <http://www.history.org/foundation/journal/summer00/yankee.cfm> March, 2012

Kibler, Luther J. *Old Powhatan, Eggleston Mansion, is Restored*, Source unknown, c1940,

Lanciano, Claude, *Our Most Skillful Architect,* Gloucester, VA: Lands End Books, 1981

Montgomery, Dennis, *(Spring 1994) Colonial Williamsburg Foundation, Colonial Williamsburg Journal* Vol. 16, No. 3 p. 14. <http://www.history.org/foundation/journal/smith.cfm> March, 2010

Oliver, Libby H. and Theobald, Mary Miley (autumn 1995) *Journal "Colonial Williamsburg."* <http://www.history.org/almanack/life/christmas/hist_candles.cfm> November, 2010

PBS – Scientific American Frontiers, (13 January, 2012), Public Broadcasting Services, <http://www.pbs.org/saf/1203/features/pocahontas.htm> January, 2012

"Powhatan Farm Receives A Certificate of Historic Merit", The Virginia Gazette (Friday, June 12, 1942)

Rasmussen, William, (1999), *Pocahontas, Her Life and Legend,* Richmond: Virginia Historical Society, Progress Printing Co., Inc.

Reese, Bill, (February 15, 1998), *Thumbnail History of the Banjo,* http://bluegrassbanjo.org/banhist.html March, 2012

Rein, Lisa, (3 September, 2007), *The Washington Post,* <http://www.washingtonpost.com/.html> January, 2012

Rickard, J, (20 June 2006), *Peninsula Campaign of 1862*, <http://www.historyofwar.org/articles/wars_Peninsula.html> January, 2011

Sayre, Brian, (September, 2010), *Williamsburg Virginia, The Manor   House,* <http://www.thorparanormal.com/williamsburg.html>   January, 2012.

Schill, Brian (01 November, 10) The American Spiritualist Movement – A Brief History from 1849 – 1920. <www.iprfinc.com/brian57.html> February, 2012

John, Emily, (April 8, 2011), *How the Civil War Changed Modern Medicine.*   <http://news.discovery.com/history/civil-war-modern-medicine-110331.html> March, 2012

Taylor, L.B. Jr., "The Ghosts of Williamsburg" Progress Printing Company, Inc. 1999

Taylor, Shawn, (2010) *Case 5.0, Manor House in Williamsburg Virginia*, <http://www.supernaturalai.com> January, 2012

Virginia Gazette, (2010), Museum on Main Features Civil War Photos, <http://www.vagazette.com/articles/2011/05/28/news/doc4ddf1dab9577b941743543.txt>

Watson, Stephanie, How EVP Works, (07 December 2004) <http://science.howstuffworks.com/science-vs-myth/afterlife/evp.htm> February, 2012.

Williams, Lloyd H., *One of Counties Oldest Farms*, Daily Press, Sunday, December 2, 1942, 10D